I0658254

Covenant of Lies

The Untold Truth!!

By Holly Spence

© 2009 by Holly Spence
Monarch Publications, LLC
monarchpublicationsllc@yahoo.com

http://www.monarchpublicationsllc.webs.com

All rights reserved. The copyright laws of the
United States of America protect this book. This
book may not be copied or reprinted for
commercial gain or profit. No part of this
publication may be reproduced or transmitted in
any form or by any means, electronic or
mechanically, including photocopy, recording or
any information storage or retrieval system now
known or to be invented, without permission in
writing from the publisher, except by a reviewer
who wishes to quote brief passages in connection
with review written for inclusion in a magazine,
newspaper or broadcast.

Monarch Publications, LLC books may be
purchased in bulk for educational, business,
fundraising or sales promotional use. For more
information, please email
monarchpublicationsllc@yahoo.com

Spence, Holly 2009
Covenant of Lies The Untold Truth/ By Holly Spence
Release 2
ISBN 978-0-578-03882-7

Edited by Melissa L. Allen
Front and back cover designed by Timothy
Hawkins

Chapters of Untold Truth

Chapters of Untold Truth

About the Author

With a passion to know, learn and live God's Word. My wife has been anointed by God to deliver His Word to His people.

A native of Cincinnati, Ohio, Holly Spence is a graduate of the School of Creative and Performing Arts in which she majored in Drama, Technical Theater Management and Vocal Music. She attended the University of Cincinnati, majoring in Chemical Technology.

She is an author *("Servant Leadership: The Heart That Serves", The Power of 10: Gaining Empowerment in 10 minutes, 10 words, 10 people)*, Conference Speaker and Workshop Facilitator. She currently serves as an OU Americas Sales LVC Program Manager for Oracle Corporation, a major Global Software Company.

My wife has a true servant's heart. She is committed to covenant relationships and has a passion for God's Word. She is a covenant member of Overflow Ministries Covenant Church where she submits and serves under the Godly government of Apostle Bennie and Pastor Delores Fluellen. She is an anointed psalmist, entrepreneur, and businesswoman. She's the mother of 3 beautiful children: Heather, Jehoshua and Joshijah-rapha. She is my best friend and covenant partner.

Vinnie C. Spence

Acknowledgements

I am simply amazed at what God has done over the past year. You are reading my third book published since the release of my first book February 28, 2008. All glory and honor belongs to God. I am grateful for what He has allowed to be produced through me.

To my top editors and critics who nothing gets published without them, Prophetess Monica Keenon (Cuz Cuz) and My Sissy, Melissa Allen I appreciate you both for continuing to take your time, to produce a quality product.

Juanita Johnson of Taylor Made Memories, LLC

Timothy Hawkins Do you see the cover? What else can be said?

Dad and Mom, thanks for your continued support and love through another project.

My Mom, thanks for your continued support.

My children thanks for making the attempt to figure out which book I am on now. Heather and Jehoshua, I am still waiting to publish your books.

To the one God has placed in my life, thanks for listening to the read through. This one was so much drama it kept you awake, didn't it?

Warning—Disclaimer

The examples in this book are fictional and not based on any person, church or corporation unless stated as an example of the life experience of the author.

Every effort was made to make this manual as complete and as accurate as possible. However, there *may be mistakes*, both typographical and in content.

Neither the author, nor publisher, shall have liability or responsibility to any person or entity with respect to real or perceived damage caused, directly or indirectly, by information contained in this book.

__Chapter One__

It was another Sunday afternoon; the vestibule of Higher Calling Christian Fellowship was full of weekly afternoon greetings. Children were running around the legs of their parents holding their Children's Church papers. Motorola, Nokia and Sidekicks were all open and being read as their owners respond to text messages that had been sent over the past three hours. Pastor Matthews and his wife stood at the front door greeting members and visitors.

Shane and Jill busted through the sanctuary doors talking and giggling as if they had not seen each other in weeks.

"Shane you are so silly, you will probably shout just like that if you would ever let go and let God".

Shane started singing "Let go and let God, Let go and let God, Let go and let God, Let Go!!!! Let Go!!! Let Go…..and let God, Oh…" Shane held on to Jill's arm and began to do his mock holy dance of his father. Shane and Jill both continued in laughter.

"Jill, you know that's my father inside and out!"

"Yeah and like I said, that's exactly what you are going to do".

"Hey, where are our parents? I am so hungry, where are we eating today?"

"Our Dads are still counting the offering, and our mothers are probably somewhere still praising God and slinging snot".

"Shane, ooh that's a visual I didn't need".

"You asked!"

"Shane and Jill sitting in the tree k.i.s.s.i.n.g...."

"B.J.! stop that, how many times do I have to tell you? Shane and I are friends."

"Well, ya'll always together like ya'll more than friends."

"Well B.J., the moment Jill becomes more than my friend, you will be the first one to know little man, give me five? Up high! Down low! Oh,

3

you're almost no longer too slow". Shane rubbed BJ on his head as he ran away.

"Shane, why did you tell him that? He will never stop."

"Aw, BJ doesn't mean any harm, besides, I meant what I said. When you become more than a friend, he will be the first to know".

"Well, I would think that I would be the first to know".

"You might be, or you might not be!" Shane began to tickle Jill.

"Stop Shane, Stop!!"

"Alright you two, where is your Dad?" said Stephanie, Shane's mother.

"I don't know, but we are hungry!"

"Well, as good as that word Pastor Matthews preached today, your hunger should be satisfied.."

"Auntie Jess, that word fed my spirit, but now I need something to feed my soul, glory, glory!!!" They all laughed at Shane.

"Jessica what do you have a taste for?" Shane chimed in, "Auntie Jess, I can have another plate of your lasagna and be satisfied". While they continued to work out the dinner menu, Mrs. Perry approached Jill about helping out with Vacation Bible School.

Mrs. Perry and Jill exchanged greetings. Mrs. Perry has always been a pillar at Higher Calling. She, along with her late husband, Calvin Perry, Jr., were two of the founding members. Mrs. Perry, a very stylish woman of her early seventies, watched both Jill and Shane grow up at Higher Calling. Mrs. Perry was their

Children's Church teacher for years. Mrs. Perry is like

a grandmother to both Jill and Shane. Since Jill's early

teenage years, Mrs. Perry had taken Jill under her wing

and mentored her as a children's church teacher, and

had helped her in so many other ways. Jill's fondness

for Mrs. Perry granted her the nickname Granny P.

"Granny P, of course I'm up for VBS this year, I'll get

Shane to do the basketball thing with the boys, we will

make it krunked) as usual." "I know you will get it

krumped!" Mrs. Perry folded her arms and threw up a

peace sign. Jill chuckled, "Granny, you are a mess! I

think Shane is rubbing off on you" "I think you are

right", Mrs. Perry laughed covering her mouth. "Jill,

every time I see you and Shane, my heart just leaps

with joy. You are growing into a fine young lady and I

think Shane is starting to see that too." "Oh Granny P,

not you too! You know Shane and I are like brother

6

and sister. It's as if we were in the womb together."

"Well honey, sometimes best friends make the best partners", she hugs Jill and kissed her on her cheek.

Mrs. Perry walked away with a slight grin on her face, knowing firsthand how Shane's affection for Jill could blossom into more. She and her late husband had been just as close as Jill and Shane. She was quite familiar with Shane's slight, but ever so present vibes of fondness toward Jill.

Jill smiled as she turned from watching Mrs. Perry walk to her car in the church parking lot. She bumped into Marcie, who is not only startled by the encounter, but also drops her bags and three bibles she is carrying. "Oh Marcie, I didn't see you. I am so sorry." Jill immediately began to pick up Marcie's belongings. With her head hung low, Marcie replied almost in a whisper, "Its okay, I know you didn't mean…." With an abrupt and condescending tone, Marcie's mother grabbed Marcie by her arm and began to scream in her face. "You clumsy idiot!" Jill looked up in disbelief and instantaneously came to Marcie's defense. "Mrs. Taylor, I bumped into Marcie. We didn't see each other". Marcie's mother continued with her insults to Marcie's face. Marcie kept her head held low to ensure her shoulder length hair would cover her embarrassed and tear stricken face. Jill stood watching Marcie and her mother walk through the parking lot. Jill couldn't hear the continued insults that Marcie was receiving, but she was humiliated for Marcie. Marcie had been a very happy and joyous child growing up in Higher

Calling. Jill and Marcie were never close, but did interact at various church functions, including teen worship and quarterly teen outings. Marcie was very outgoing until about a couple of years ago. Everything seemed to change after her father lost his job as a high power stockbroker. He was with his firm for twenty-five years and was let go. It was never determined exactly what happened, but there were rumors of some improprieties. The family went missing for a few months. Marcie and her mom returned to church, but it was clear that things had declined in their home. Marcie wasn't her talkative, joyous self. She was constantly by her mother's side and they no longer remained after service to fellowship. Mrs. Taylor didn't participate in women's ministry or with the youth ministry. The family seemed to be so withdrawn,

even after Mr. Taylor returned to services weekly;
there hadn't been any involvement from the
Taylor family, of late, at Higher Calling.

Chapter Two

Marcie slid into the back of the family's Mercedes E-320, which was a down size from the previous G-550 SUV. The Taylor family was struggling financially, comparatively speaking. Since Mr. Taylor's two-year layoff, the family's million-dollar income had been reduced to less than half. The Mercedes and hillside mansion had been sustained because of wise investments and Mr. Taylor's need to keep up appearances. But the

Taylor's home was far from the host of bi-weekly dinner parties, valet parking and annual employee Christmas gatherings it had once been. The French garden along the east side of the estate was now overgrown with local weeds. The front yard gets cut only after threats of fines from the local village administration. Mrs. Taylor does her laundry only once a week; two hours on Friday evening. If an article of clothing doesn't make the weekly designated two hours, consider it dirty another week. Marcie learned this the hard way after having to wear a soiled uniform shirt to school for the whole week. She was grateful *that* was her last week at her private school, but the public school scrutiny wasn't much better. Mrs. Taylor consigned all of her St. John clothing, with the exception of a couple of showpieces, all of which could be interchanged and made into four to five different outfits. Her jewelry had been auctioned off, along with her special ordered Jaguar XL. This was all done at the direction and insistence of Mr. Taylor, who used his corrupt connections with an auction house to give the appearance that the donations were for charity, but he actually received an under the table kick back. This was done to stay afloat and keep the appearances that the great Calvin Taylor had not hit rock bottom. However, the tomato soup and crackers for dinner told another story. The empty rooms that once held exquisite antiques and original works of Van Gogh were all now shut off and never entered. However, the bar didn't seem to lack replenishing. Mr. Taylor found himself at the bottom of a vodka bottle at least two to three times a week.

As Marcie shut the door, her father's booming
voice bounced off the windows, "What the hell
were the two of you doing?" Selma
unintentionally began to stutter over her own
words. Marcie thought that even though her
mother was delayed in her response she would be
safe, since they were so close to church. Surely
her father wouldn't risk being seen. Before Marcie
could finish her thought, Calvin's hand lunged to
the passenger side of the car and back at his side
all before the first stop light. The force of Calvin's
so-called wave was so powerful, Selma Taylor's
face was plastered against the window with about
a half dollar sized blood pool. "Look what you
have done now!! You have smeared the window
with your blood, clean it up, you imbecile. I don't

14

know why I stay with you, putting up with your nonsense! When I say we are to leave immediately after church, we are to leave immediately after church. No delays, do you hear me? Do you hear me Selma? Answer, you stupid…" Selma answered as she held back tears and wiped her face, "I understand. I was helping Marcie pick up our bibles she dropped." Calvin's voice rang with fury, "Oh, please don't blame Marcie for your inability to follow instructions; Always passing the buck!" Marcie wasn't surprised by her mother's attempt to throw her under the bus, she almost didn't blame her. She was just trying to relieve the attention from herself. Nevertheless, that same action made Marcie bitter and angry inside. She desperately needed protection and love, not more exposure to this self-serving parenting.

Calvin's anger suddenly turned as it always does. "Marcie, if you would have been in the car, it would have never happened; you were right behind me. What delayed your slow tail?" Marcie wanted to yell back so badly "…it wouldn't have happened if I wouldn't have been waiting for your good for nothing two timing wife!" But Marcie simply replied, "I am so sorry Daddy, it won't happen again."

Surprisingly, that's all it took this afternoon to relinquish Calvin's grip of terror on Marcie. Calvin returned to focus on Selma, "Do you see that Selma? Marcie accepts her errors and is willing to please. You, on the other hand, always have excuses, you stupid B…" the phone rang, Calvin always keeps his phone on auto answer. "Hello, this is Cal Taylor. Hey man, oh yea, I am all in tonight… I'm there; Alright, talk with you then". The rest of the ride for the Taylors is one of silence and relief for Marcie. She laid her head back and wished she could wake-up from this nightmare.

<u>Chapter Three</u>

Shane walked up behind Jill, and poked her in

both sides with his fingers. Jill let out a loud

screech, "Shane!" Shane held his head back in

laughter. Jill's parents along with Shane's parents

witnessed the whole event. "He got you honey,

didn't he?" "Yes, Daddy he did," said Jill.

Jessica announced, "Well, we have decided to go

to Engine 13. I've called ahead for seating and we

18

are scheduled for 3:30 p.m." Engine 13 was a local restaurant that was a converted Firehouse; this was a regular, after church, dinner spot. Several well known Pastors, as well as Gospel and R&B artists could be seen here any given week. "Good Jessica, that gives me time to go home and climb out of this suit." "Aw Dad, do we have to make that stop?" said Shane.

"Son, I do not want to sit up there looking F.U.B.O", "What? Dad do you mean F.U.B.U?" "No, I mean F.U.B.O, Fine, Uncomfortable, Black and Overdressed." Everyone erupted in laughter, with the exception of Shane, who threw his face into his hands and shook his head back and forth. Shane's father, Henry McFinley, is a very good-looking man. He is six foot five, smooth brown skinned and clean cut. He and Stephanie have been married almost 21 years. Carl and Jessica

Richardson have also been married almost 21

years; their anniversaries are only separated by a

month. The foursome, were high school sweet

hearts who planned their weddings and vacations

together. Therefore, no one was surprised when

both Stephanie and Jessica announced that they

were pregnant at about the same time.

"Yes, Henry you are fine!!" said his wife

Stephanie. Henry threw his arms around Stephanie

and said, "See if you let me go home and change

you can see…" Jill covered her ears and opened

her mouth in laughter all at the same time; Shane

repeatedly shoved his index finger in his mouth

indicating his displeasure of his father's public

display of affection. Carl and Jessica both

commented at the same time "Get a room!" Henry told Carl, "Man, you can go home and change your clothes too, we have time." They both high fived each other as Jill chimed in, "Daddy, please don't respond. Seeing Aunt Stephanie and Uncle Henry is hard enough to swallow." Jessica patted Jill on her shoulder as if she was assuring her that won't happen.

"Well, I'm going to go with Aunt Jess and Uncle Carl while you two love birds, go home. "Is that okay?" "Shane, you know you don't have to ask," said Jessica. Carl commented to Henry, "*Stephanie* is really raising a gentleman." "What are you saying, man?" as Henry put his fists up to fight. Stephanie and Jessica looked at each other and shook their heads, "Boys will be boys,"

Jessica looked on as Carl and Henry shadow box in the church parking lot. Carl and Henry hug. "Alright now, we will see you in a minute," said Carl.

Henry hit the remote on their loaded black Lexus. Stephanie snuggled into the comfortable caramel leather seats. "Henry, are you seeing what I am seeing?" Henry answered as if he was not aware of Stephanie's observations. "What do you see babe; not another diamond is it?" Stephanie Richardson was well known for her exquisite taste of diamonds and has had most of her jewelry custom made from the diamond district in NYC to the designers of South Africa. Henry spared no expense on his wife of 20 plus years. Dr. Stephanie McFinley held her PhD in psychology and had been blessed with a very lucrative

practice. However, Stephanie had always been

humble and very grateful to God for the life she

had been afforded to live.

"No, not another diamond, but my precious son

has eyes for little Jill. They are like brother and

sister, but that's what usually happens when you

are that close…you remember how it was for us?"

Stephanie continued to reflect and make

comments on Shane's looks and extra attention he

ha been paying Jill. Henry rode in silence, just

listening to his wife. He hoped that he wouldn't

have to engage in conversation regarding this

matter. Stephanie had mentioned this before and

Henry had done well to stay away from the

subject. He knew it was only a matter of time

before he would have to discuss it, but he was

thankful that it wouldn't be today.

Chapter Four

Shane jumped into the back seat of the

Richardson's 135i convertible BMW. Carl let the

top down at Jill's prompting. The car was filled

with laughter as Carl tells his latest arsenal of

jokes. Carl was well known for his jokes; Jessica

jumped in every now and then with a joke of her

own. She often got the punch line wrong, which

added another level of humor and laughter. As a

result, Jessica herself often became the brunt of the jokes.

"So Shane, you have one more year of school, have you decided where you are going? If you make your decision, I believe Jill will make hers. And then, I will know how much I am going to be out a year?" "Daddy!!" squealed Jill. "Uncle Carl, you think she's waiting on me? I'm actually waiting on her. I've been approached by Penn State and Stanford, but I don't want to be on the opposite coast of Jill." "Do you hear that honey, Shane is waiting on Jill to make a decision, isn't young love grand?" Carl teased. "Daddy, not you too!? Everyone lately, particularly today, seems to be commenting on our relationship status. What is with that?" Jill chuckles. Jill's mother, Jessica wasted no time to take the opportunity to chime in, attempting to steer the conversation away from the thought of Shane and Jill being an official item. "You know Daddy likes to have fun. He didn't mean anything by it. Everyone knows you two have been together since you came out of the womb, and that you are the best of friends." "I *do* like to have fun, but I wasn't born yesterday, and I *know* what I see," said Carl. Jill was no completely embarrassed. "Daddy! You are talking like Shane and I aren't sitting in the back seat!!! *Please!!!*" Carl continued with his thoughts of this blossoming relationship and gave his stamp of approval. Jessica, on the other hand, continued to comment against the relationship and continued to redirect the conversation to Jill and Shane being friends. Jill was glad to hear that her mother had her back on this one. When Shane was asked about his uncharacteristic silence, he brushed it off with a witty response that caused the whole car to laugh, but Shane didn't join in the folly.

Carl, Jessica, Jill and Shane all arrived at Engine 13 Restaurant. There were several groups standing outside talking and continuously checking their pagers to see if it had vibrated. The converted firehouse was very deceiving as it relates to size. From the outside, it appeared that the restaurant didn't seat any more than 50-60 people at one time. However, the restaurant was very deep, actually having the ability to accommodate over 300 guests at one time. *Richardson and Associates* often held their employee Christmas parties at Engine 13. Although others had to wait, Carl had favor with the management of Engine 13. The staff knew to sit the Richardson party immediately upon arrival.

Carl parked the car and proceeded to let the host know that his party had arrived. As Carl walked in, you could hear the various staff members give their hellos. "Hello Mr. Richardson," "Welcome back Mr. Richardson..." Before Carl got to the host's desk, a very enthusiastic inquiry was made of Carl. "Hello Mr. Richardson. How many are in your party today?" "Well, hello Brandy, there will be six. I knew the reason I missed you in church was because you were working." "Mr. Richardson, you know you can count on it. Anytime you don't see me in service, I am working! We are clearing your table now." Carl thanked Brandy as he scans the restaurant to see if he recognized colleagues or other church members in the crowd. Carl had to look between trays of food as the wait staff moved through the restaurant, as if they had power boosters built in the heels of their shoes. The clattering of silverware and plates filled the air along with the laughter and whispers of conversations. Even in this loud atmosphere, a very familiar laugh continued to rise to the top of the noise, which caused Carl to scan the restaurant several times to locate the origin.

Carl noticed a small gathering around the bar and the source of the laughter. There were two men sitting on the bar stools with three others standing behind them. There was one stool that was not in his view. Just then, one of the men standing shifted and he could see a woman's head tilt back in laughter. As she turns her head, Carl and Beverly's eyes meet. In that moment, Carl wished his curiosity wouldn't have gotten the best of him. Beverly raised her drink to acknowledge Carl and blew a seductive air kiss. Carl turned to make his exit and there stood, Jessica with everyone. Jessica immediately noticed that Carl was startled upon seeing her enter the restaurant. "Well Carl, why are you standing there looking like you swallowed the canary?" Henry, knowing his friend much longer then Jessica, immediately bailed him out with "You sure do, and you didn't *save me any?*" Jessica and Stephanie laughed just as the hostess bellowed, "Richardson party of 6, your table is ready."

As they moved to their table, Carl was very intentional about where he looked in the restaurant, planning not to make any additional eye contact with Beverly.

Chapter Five

The waitress stood at the table and asked if anyone

was interested in dessert. Carl, who always wanted

dessert after eating the five-alarm gumbo,

declined. Everyone was shocked, to say the least.

This was the last sign Jessica needed to confirm

that something was definitely bothering Carl.

While Jessica analyzed Carl, Jill continually tried

to engage Shane in conversation, as she did all

during dinner. Shane repeatedly gave her short,

one-word answers. When Jill inquired of Shane's shortness in speech, he would disregard her question with the wave of his hand or by joking with the others at the table. When the check came to the table, Carl and Henry had their usual debate about who was going to pay. Jessica and Stephanie announced that they were going to the boutique next door. Jill and Shane followed behind their mothers.

Shane told his mom he was going the opposite direction to visit the Sharper Image store. Jill was happy to tag along to find out what in the world was wrong with Shane. They hadn't split from their mothers 30 seconds when Jill, with a big sigh said, "OK, what is going on with YOU! You barely had two words to say to me throughout dinner. I ask you questions and you either blew me off or completely ignored me…" As Jill continued, she was actually getting very irritated the more she thought about Shane's behavior. "…I can't believe you would actually do that to me! We've had disagreements, but never have you absolutely ignored me; not even when I went to the eighth grade spring fling with Jimmy Parsons." Shane continued to walk, still not acknowledging Jill, as if he didn't hear her at all. "OH SHANE! This is just childish, will you tell me what is wrong…what have I done?" Without warning and completely catching Jill off guard, Shane turned to Jill and quickly, but gently placed each of her ears between both his thumbs and index fingers. He pulled her toward him and planted the longest kiss on Jill's plump lips. Jill was in complete shock, standing on her tiptoes, arms hanging in the air in the traditional surrender pose and eyes wide open. Shane finally opened his eyes and released Jill's lips. With her face still cradled in his hands, Shane looked at her once, blinked and gingerly planted another kiss on Jill's lips. Still looking into Jill's eyes, he released her, , and then turned and continued to walk down the sidewalk with his hand in his pants pockets, not saying a word.

While Henry and Carl were arguing about the bill, a Firehouse Molten Brownie was brought to the table by their waitress. Henry said "We didn't order this dessert." "Oh, I know it's for Mr. Richardson from the lady at the bar." Henry leaned back in his chair and slightly nodded his head, "Oh, so *that's* what's wrong with you! You were obviously distracted during dinner. I did my best man to keep the pressure off of you, but hawk eye Jessica was all over you." "I know. I appreciate it, said Carl." "OK, so who did you see? Who is this dessert from? How awkward would that have been if the dessert had shown up while everyone was still here? Oh I don't even want to imagine Jessica's reaction. But I would be more concerned with the reaction of the kids....so who is the lady at the bar?" Just then, a tall, slender, dark, smooth skin, middle-aged woman walked over; as heads turned with every step she made toward the table. Beverly Martinez, ESQ., stood at the table with a hand blown Engine 13 red wine glass in her left hand. She was wearing a low cut, form fitting black dress. Her neck was adorned with a simple strain of fresh water pearls and 3 inch Stuart Weitzman pumps. "Hello Carl, I thought you could enjoy some dessert after dinner with the family."

"Hello Beverly, I am stuffed, but maybe it would have been something we could have shared if it arrived earlier," said Carl. "Well maybe you can have your dessert to go..." Beverly then picked up the fork from the table and stuck it in the chocolate dessert. Chocolate was hanging from the fork. Then, Beverly slowly, and with much seduction, put the cake in her mouth all without losing eye contact with Carl. Beverly left the table saying her hello to Henry by name and winking at Carl. She walked back across the restaurant shaking the fork back and forth in her right hand.

Chapter Six

After arriving home Marcie immediately made a
bee line for her room, always leaving the door
open. This was once her place of security and
solitude, but that was no longer the case. To
ensure she wouldn't catch the cross fire of her
father's fury, Marcie retreated to the overgrown
east estate garden. There she would dig up her
journal and proceed to the algae infested lake.
Once there, Marcie sat down on the dock swinging
her legs back and forth dreaming of happier days

and losing hope that her future could ever hold any pleasure. Marcie was not just active in church, but also in school, running on the track team, singing in the school chorale and participating in swim team. Academically, she has always been the head of her class. She's also a star athlete. Marcie's days were filled with practice and preparation for weekend meets and competitions. Her wall was full of ribbons, trophies and medals of her athletic accomplishments. The lack of involvement for Marcie has been a devastating blow for her. She often romanced her thoughts of days gone by.

Marcie remembered the days when she would run through the house with her father chasing her, having innocent father -daughter bonding, which she longed for again. Her Dad would come in her room and play tea party. While her mother wouldn't allow her to have real tea, her Dad would make sure Chiquita, the housekeeper, would make a pot when he was planning to attend. Marcie smiled as she was reminded of her father bringing in her mother's Wedgewood teapot and a plate of perfectly wedged cut lemons for their party. As the wind rolled off the lake, the air whisked against Marcie's face. Marcie reclinedwith her back on the dock thinking, "Wow, those were the days."

Marcie remembered her mother's jovial smile and warm loving arms of affection. Those times of affection are also scattered with the wind. Marcie rolled over on her stomach on the dock to write in

41

her journal when she heard a scream of horror.

Marcie immediately jumped to her feet running

toward the sound of the screams. Her heart raced,

not knowing what she would find; she could see

flickers of memories of her mother and her life, as

she knew it, in her mind. The only thing moving

faster than her legs was her mind, trying to figure

out what could be wrong. Just as she rounded the

south end of the estate, her worst fears were

confirmed. There her mother was, covered in

blood. Marcie screamed "Momma, Momma, Oh

My God No! No! No! No!"

Chapter Seven

Stephanie and Jessica hadhit most of the boutiques near the restaurant and had the bags to prove it. They been friends since high school, when Jessica moved with her family from Montana. The two, just as with their children, are practically inseparable. They continued into the fifth store laughing and making big "to do's" over the new spring line of shoes the boutique was carrying. The store clerk approached and Jessica immediately began to point out the shoes she waned to try on. "Jess, that's too many pairs of shoes; like you really need them" said Stephanie. Jessica was quick to come back. "Stephanie I know you are not calling the kettle black? You know a lady could never have too many shoes…" Just then, Stephanie jumped up with a high pitch "Oh! Do you see this?!!" It's a burnt orange ankle strap with a rhinestone encrusted stiletto heel. Jess replied with a gasping "Jesus! Keep me near the cross…" Stephanie was quick to point out that she saw it first, and it would be hers, regardless of the sizes available. They both laughed.

Jessica said to Stephanie, "Hey Stephanie, You know who I have really been thinking of for the past month?" Stephanie replied, "No, who?" "Selma Taylor, what can we do to help her?"

44

Stephanie stretched her neck and rubbed her temples. "Jessica, Selma has to want our help first. I don't think based on what I have observed that she is seeking help." Jessica unwilling to take that as a final answer said, "I believe we should at least reach out to her and allow her to reject us. She needs to know that there is a way of escape. I know you are far more the expert in this area Dr. McFinley, but I just think we are wrong to see her in need and not reach out." Stephanie cleared her throat and began hurling the statistics of women in bad relationships and all her text book knowledge, giving further justification on why this was not the time to intervene. Jessica was not having it and compelled Stephanie to agree to talk to Selma with her. Stephanie finally agreed, but not without making her final case and warning Jessica that it could be like running into a brick wall. Jessica agreed.

Stephanie then batted her eyes and said, "Jess, have you noticed our two offspring?" Knowing full well what Stephanie meant, Jessica still choe to act ignorant to her suggestion. "I mean have you noticed how Shane has been looking at Jill. I think he likes her." Jessica didn't comment. She stood up and looked at the fourth pair of shoes she had tried on. Jessica said, "Stephanie, what do you think of this shoe? Girl, isn't it sharp?"

Stephanie found it strange that Jessica didn't respond, but after all, she was indulging in one of her favorite activities, shoe shopping. "I think they look good, girl and I also think Shane and Jill look good together." "Yes, they are sweet kids, but honey they have been together since they were born into this world." Stephanie, taken aback at this point, "You can't tell me you don't see how Shane looks at her or is this your way of saying you don't approve?" "Oh Stephanie, I am saying that they are friends, nothing more. I am sure that's the last thing on their minds. They have school to finish and then there is college. They have their lives ahead of them. There is so much for them both to experience." With her arms folded and clearly not happy with Jessica Stephanie said, "Well, you don't approve! What is that about? Surely, you are not saying Shane is not good enough!!" "Oh, you know I am not saying that. I *am* saying that they should..." Stephanie interrupted, "Jessica, I know you and this avoidance and reluctance to answer me directly is your standard M.O.! I don't know what your problem is with Shane, but I believe that they would make a wonderful couple. Furthermore, they are perfect. They know each other, similar to how we know each other. And,what better covenant to have established between our seed? What is wrong with you!!?" Jessica definitely didn't think that she would receive such a direct confrontation from Stephanie on this matter She didn't want to continue the conversation, but she didn't want Stephanie mad at her either.

"Stephanie, I'm sorry, I didn't mean to get you so upset...it's just that..." "It's what Jessica? I'mnot Carl and you can't avoid your way out of the conversation!" Jessica snapped her head, "What!? I know you are not Carl and I don't do that to him." "Girl please, did you forget who you are talking to?" "Stephanie, this is not the appropriate place to continue this conversation, since you have taken it to a whole new level!" Still very direct and very upset, Stephanie replied, "Jessica, you are right, but based on your reaction today, maybe its best that we don't finish this conversation!" Jessica planned to respond, but Carl and Henry came through the door. Stephanie grabbe her bags and stormed toward the door. "Henry, I'm ready to go!" Stephanie exited without purchasing one shoe. Henry and Carl look at each other and instantly they read each other's mind. They repeat together "Oh boy, terrible, just terrible!" They snicker, but make sure their wives don'thear. "Well Carl, and Jessica, it appears that our afternoon together has come to an end. You both

49

enjoy your evening. Carl, I'll holler at ya man!"
They say their good-byes.

Carl,standing above Jessica, waits for an explanation, butJessica doesn't say a word. She continued shopping as if nothing had happened. She had the sales clerk ring up all six pairs of shoes, and her first word to Carl is, "Honey can you go ahead and pay for that while I get my things together?" Carl moved to the counter and handled the $687.23 Sunday afternoon shopping bill Jessica had quickly accumulated. As the sales clerk was bagingg the newly purchased shoes, Carl took the opportunity to probe Jessica, since she was obviously not volunteering any information. "So Jessica, what happened between you and Stephanie?" "Oh nothing. She will cool off and we'll go about, as if nothing has happened." "Jessica, the two of you don't have spats like that, what happened?" Jessica replied nonchalantly, "Oh, she mentioned something about Shane liking Jill, and I just said that they are friends and they have their whole lives ahead of them. Well, she took that to mean that I didn't think Shane was good enough for Jill. I wasn't saying that at all. I just don't think we should force them into anything they don't want to do. We should encourage them to finish school, travel, and enjoy life. They are so young, no need to complicate life with a relationship neither of them is ready for." "Well Jess, no wonder she is upset!" said Carl. Jessica still appearing as if she has done nothing wrong, "What?" Carl was in disbelief. "Jessica what is it about Jill and Shane being a couple you just don't want to face? Is it the fact that this is your only child? I would think that you would be happy that Shane has his eye on Jill. What more could a parent ask than for their daughter to have a young man like Shane? This is every Christian parent's dream; a nice believer for their daughter. Not only have we known him since his conception, we've known his parents. And, I knew his grandparents before him. Jessica, you should be ashamed…that was a slap in Stephanie's face." "Oh, Carl please don't you be so dramatic!" Jessica, having becomeirritated with Carl, grabbed her bags and stormed out of the boutique.

Chapter Eight

Henry waved for Shane to meet them in the car. Stephanie walked beside Henry with a mission to leave the boutique as quickly as possible. Her every step telling of her frustration she has just experienced with her best friend . When Henry and Stephanie arrived at the car, Henry sat down and shut the door, Stephanie bounced in the seat and shut the Lexus door. as if it was a 1962 Ford Truck. Henry cringed on the inside, but dared not say a word. Henry knew Stephanie very well, so with caution he asked "Do you want to talk about it?" Just then, Shane hopped in the back seat and he looked like a nine year old boy who had lost his first puppy. Meanwhile, Stephanie sits in the front seat looking as if she is ready for a mafia war. It was at that point, Henry knew that he had a mess on his hands. With little humor, he said, "What in the world has happened between the last morsel of dinner and a walk around the boutiques?" But, there's still utter silence in the car. Henry continues, "Well does anyone want to talk about what is bothering them? The last I saw the two of you, you were happy-go-lucky with no cares in the world, and now Shane you look as if the world has crashed on you; and your mother is mad that it did!" Still, there was no word from either of them. "Okay, so it's going to be the silent treatment. Well, when you are ready to talk I am here; that goes for both of you." The McFinley family rode home in silence. As she thinks about what's just happened, Stephanie can't figure out if she'sreally upset with Jessica, or just hurt. As tears rolled down her face, she tried to wipe them so Henry doesn't see them. She felt his gentle hand on her leg. Stephanie continued to look out the window and wipe her tears. She placed her left hand on Henry's hand welcoming the intended consolation.

As they arrive home, Henry pulled into the circular drive, Shane finally said,. "Dad I will get out here!" "Ok, sure son!" replied Henry. Henry asked Stephanie if she would like to get out, but she didn't say a word and didn't move. Henry waited for a moment and then pulled the car into the garage. He got out of the car and opened the door for Stephanie. He extended his hand to help her out of the car. Stephanie grabbed her Dolce and Gabanna handbag and took Henry by the hand. Henry slowly walked along the path at the side of the house with Stephanie and whispered, whispers, "So babe, are you ready to talk? What happened with you and Jessica?" Stephanie, with tears in her eyes, and in a cracked voice replied, "I can't believe Jessica! I just can't believe her! Henry I don't want Shane to hear us." "Don't worry, he's in the house" said Henry. Jessica continued, "I asked Jessica what she thought about Shane and Jill being a couple." Henry's heart dropped. Of all the things they could have been arguing about, Henry hoped that it wouldn't be about this. He had successfully stayed away from giving his opinion on this issue, and now the time had come. He was going to be forced to give his thoughts on the one subject he had successfully avoided. "Jessica just blew it off and I didn't think anything of it, and then as I explained further what I was seeing, she totally dismissed it and was obviously more interested in purchasing another pair of shoes, that she doesn't need! I just couldn't believe it. Henry, I initially just looked past her nonchalant attitude, but I know Jessica; that type of avoidance is typical of her when she doesn't agree with something or someone." Henry with hesistated and then spoke, "Well Steph, look at it from her perspective. This is her only child..." Henry says this with sympathy, "It's my only child also, I mean, Henry you weren't there, and she practically implied that Shane wasn't good enough! I just lost it then." "Oh come on Stephanie, I am sure that's not the case at all. Jessica has known Shane all of his life. Jessica just wants Jill to concentrate on her schooling. I am sure that's what she wants for the both of them. The two of them have grown up more like brother and sister anyway. It would be a little strange...." Stephanie interrupted Henry and has a look of disbelief, "So what is it with you two? You are not for it either?" "Honey, I didn't say that...I just..." Stephanie interrupted Henry again, "I know you too Henry, and this poor attempt you are making to understand how Jessica is feeling isn't flying with me." "Stephanie, I was just trying to give you another perspective, Shane doesn't even look at

Jill that way." "Henry George McFinley! You have to be kidding me. There is no way that you can sit across from me and tell me you don't see how your son looks at Jill? Honey, it's more than brother and sister in the Lord. He likes that young lady! And, you and Jessica better come out of your fantasy world. Ask him; ask him Henry! Find out for yourself." Henry tilts his head to the side and says, "I don't want to put anything in his head or force an idea on him that's not there." Stephanie let out a loud sarcastic laugh, "Are you kidding me? Oh let's just stop now, this conversation has to come to an end." Stephanie grabbed her bag and walked back around the house. Henry called out to her "Stephanie! Stephanie!", but there was no answer.

Chapter Nine

Marcie held her bloody mother in her arms as
Selma screamed in pain. Marcie didn't know
where her father was, but knew she had to get
medical attention for her mother. "Mommy, I
don't want to leave you, but I have to call 911."
There was no response from Selma. Marcie laid
her mother down slowly and darted toward the
house to call 911. Marcie had no idea what the
inside of the cold mansion would hold. Would her
father be standing at the door? Would his fury be

unleashed on her? Marcie was willing to take the risk. She couldn't let her mother lay there. Marcie stepped into the front door, which had been left open; she immediately looked around to ensure she wouldn'tbe ambushed by her own father. Marcie ran to the kitchen and picked up the phone to dial 911. The operator answered, "911 what is your emergency?" Marcie, in a frantic and quite voice said "Yes, this is Marcie Taylor; I need an ambulance at 45 Grand Maple Drive." The operator responded, "Okay, how many people are injured?" "It's one person. It is my mother. I don't know what happened, she is covered in blood, please hurry, hurry." "OK, the ambulance has already been dispatched, is she breathing?" In a high pitch voice Marcie answers, "I don't know, I had to leave her outside to make the call, please

have them hurry. I need to go back outside to my
mom." The operator reassured Marcie that the
ambulance was on the way and she should go back
out to her mother. Marcie ran back to her Mom,
thinking about where her Dad could be. She
didn't know if he had left or was still in the house.
When Marcie arrived at her mother's side, she
found that her mother was no longer conscious..
"Mommy! Mommy! Can you hear me? Can you
hear me? Oh God, NO!!! NO!!! NO!!! NO!!!!
Mommy!!!" The ambulance sirens could be heard
under Marcie's screaming. The paramedics
jumped from the ambulance with their required
equipment. "What happened, and what is the
victim's name?" said the paramedic. "I don't
know. I heard her screaming and found her
covered in blood. After I called 911 and came

back out I saw that she wasn't . Her name is Selma, Selma Taylor". One paramedic continued to work on Mrs. Taylor. He checked her vitals and tried to revive her while his partner tried to get as much information as possible from Marcie. "What is your relationship to the victim?" "I am her daughter" said Marcie. The paramedic starte to ask Marcie again what happened. At that point, Mrs. Taylor regained consciousness. "Mrs. Taylor, stay with us. Do you know where you are hurt?" Selma began to call out for Marcie. Marcie replied, "I'mhere Mommy." "Marcie honey, I am so sorry, I am so sorry you have to go through this." Marcie simply replied with "I love you Mommy!" The paramedics returned with the gurney and prepared to transport Mrs. Taylor to North General Hospital.

The paramedics got Mrs. Taylor on the gurney and helpd Marcie in the back of the cab as well. Selma had an oxygen mask on her and she was going in and out. The paramedic was monitoring her very closely. "Hi, my name is Marcus, what's your name?" "Marcie" said in a soft voice. "Well, it is nice to meet you Marcie. What happened here Marcie?" Marcie began to cry as she held her mother's hand. "I don't know. I was at the lake when I heard the screams from my mother." "Marcie, I do know that these wounds are not self inflicted. Do you know who did this to your mother?" Marcie, with her head hung low started to cry harder. Marcus just patted Marcie on her back and said, "When we get to the hospital, I'll make sure there is someone there for you to talk to."

The paramedics cut the sirens as they arrived at North General, doctors and nurses ran to meet the paramedics. An emergency doctor bellows, "What do we have here?" "Victim that has been severely beaten, sustained severe and numerous external injuries; could be some internal bleeding. Blood pressure is stable at 120/30, heart 50..." The nurse asked "What's the patient's name and is there a next of kin to contact?" Marcus replied, "...this is her daughter Marcie." "OK, Marcie, come with me. yYou can't go back there..." Marcie is unresponsive to the nurses directions. The nurse guided her to another area where they could talk. "Marcie, my name is Courtney. I am a nurse here at North General.

What happened with your mom?" Marcie was motionless, as she stared off into space. Courtney could see that Marcie's clothes and arms were blood stained. "Marcie, let's take you back and get you cleaned up…you're not hurt are you?" Marcie was speechless. She followed Courtney as she led her to a room where she could get cleaned up. "Marcie, I know you may be in shock right now, but if you have any information concerning what has happened to your mother it will help us in helping her…" just then Marcie broke down in tears. Courtney was caught completely off guard. Courtney tried desperately to hold Marcie up as she got her to a private area. Courtney rocked Marcy back and forth attempting to comfort her.

Courtney is not sure about what has happened, but she can't help but think this situation looked so recognizable to her. Courtney had seen a lot at North General emergency, but her personal experience of bringing her mother in to the same emergency room at Marcie's age was all too familiar.

<u>Chapter Ten</u>

After storming out of the boutique, Jessica made

her way to the car. Jill was already leaning on the

outside of the car still in disbelief about what had

occurred between her and Shane. Jill noticede her

mother's obvious anger, it showed in her body

language and was all over her face. Jill thought

that her Mom's obvious angry was definitely more

important than her personal plight. "Mom, what's

wrong?" Jessica closed her eyes and shook her

head, "It's nothing dear, just a little disagreement

I've had." "Well you look as if it was more than a disagreement…wheere's Daddy?" just as she asked, Jill could see her Dad with three shopping bags of shoes. Jill with a smirk said, "Is this the disagreement." Jessica couldn't hold her anger long. She was so amused that Jill would think that buying shoes would cause such a disappointing disposition in her. How Jessica wished that was what it was. She didn't want Jill to know the real reason for her look of disappointment. "Jill, you know shoes are a girls best friend." Jessica hugged Jill. "Daddy, do you need some help?" Jill proceeded to meet her dad to help out. "Thanks baby girl." Carl and Jessica's eyes met. Carl gave Jessica another look of disapproval. Jessica immediately looked away. Carl unlocked the car and popped the trunk. Carl placed the packages he and Jill have been carrying in the trunk. "Jessica, do you want to put those packages in the trunk?" Jessica broughts her bags to the trunk and instantly moved to the passenger's side for the ride home all without saying a word. The family rode through the parking lot of the restaurant without a word. Jill gazed out of the back seat window still in shock over her encounter with Shane. He'd never expressed his feelings, where did that kiss come from, thought Jill. In an effort to drown out her thoughts, she asked her father to turn on some music. Jill's father obliged andthe smooth sounds of Chris Botti played *"When I Fall In Love"* through the speakers. Jill popped off the back seat in a slight panic, "No Daddy! Please change that! "OK, baby girl, calm down." Carl changed the disc, *"Grateful"* by Hezekiah Walker came on.

"That's better Daddy, thanks!" "Sure sweetie."

Carl couldn't help but think "who was she afraid

of falling in love with." He knew all too well there

was something definitely there between Shane and

Jill. Carl understood her apprehension. She and

Shane were as close as brother and sister. So now

engaging in a relationship, would that put things at

jeopardy? Carl thought that would be an easier

issue to deal with than Jessica's reaction to this

seemly budding relationship. One thing Carl knew

Jessica had to deal with whatever her concern was

with Shane.

Carl finally broke the silence and asked "Is anyone

up for ice cream?" Jessica declined, as he thought,

but Jill said, "I am up for a scoop or two."

"Alright thenn it's a date, we will take Mom home

and go out for ice cream." The Richardsons arrivd
home. Carl told Jessica that he would bring the
packages in upon his return. Jessica said that she
would go ahead and take in what she could carry
now. Carl offered to help, but Jessica declined, as
she often did when she was in this space of
irritation.

"OK baby girl, it's just you and me. Jump up
front! What flavor do you think it will be today?
Vanilla and Chocolate? Butter Pecan? What's
your delight?" asked Carl. "Daddy, right now I
wish I could have all the flavors." "Well, that
sounds like you need to talk. What happened after
dinner, did I miss something?"

While Jill was comfortable talking to her Dad about everything, she wasn't exactly comfortable telling him that she received her first kiss today, and that it was from Shane, who planted the longest passionate kiss on her lips. Jill was feeling as if this was too much to handle. "Daddy, its Shane! When we left church everything was just fine. The ride over you started talking about us having a relationship and by the time we got to dinner, he was totally ignoring me. He never said a word, even when I asked him after dinner. I told him that he didn't even treat me this bad when I went to the eighth grade spring fling with Jimmy Parsons." Carl wasn't surprised at all, but he wondered *"could Jill not see that Shane was interested in her"*. Carl answered his own question in his head. He was glad that Jill didn't recognize this; she didn't have experience with boys even at the age of seventeen. "Honey, haven't you noticed at all that Shane has been treating you differently; maybe showing a little more interest or different type of interest?" "Oh Daddy, I don't know, everyone else seems to be noticing it…am I the only one that's missing it?" Jill hearing her father asks these questions, felt a light bulb going off on the inside of her.

Carl and Jill arrived at the local ice cream parlor. In shock and disbelief, Jill asked, "Daddy do you think Shane likes me?" Carl looked at Jill over the car, "Honey, let's order our ice cream and then have a sit down." Jill ran to the other side of the car and hugged her Dad. As they waited in line Jill continued to prod her father. "Daddy, so do you think Shane likes me? Do you?" Carl ordered his ice cream "A double scoop of black walnut please. Baby girl, what are you having?" Jill said "Two scoops of cookies and crème. Daddy, you didn't answer me, you know Shane has already ignored me today, not you too!" Carl chuckled, "Honey, yes I believe that Shane likes you. I should be grateful that you missed this all together. It confirms that you don't have your head wrapped up in boys and you have your priorities straight, as we have raised you to do. God first, and everything else will follow." "Well, if that's how he feels, why didn't he just say that?" Carl chuckled again, "OK, I am sure your mother would say *"the brain is just not the same"* meaning men and women think differently. He probably has said it indirectly. "But Daddy, we talk about everything, so what makes this so different?" Carl answered, "This is VERY different. He has to share his inner personal thoughts and those inner personal thoughts are about you. Rolls of many thoughts are probably going through his head." Jill still not quite understanding thinking that Shane should be able to say whatever is on his mind. "But Dad, he tells me everything else, I would think this would be easier. We have been friends forever!" "You got it baby girl, it's just that. You have been friends forever and he has to take that into consideration. Shane has to consider that if he puts his feelings on the line, will you reject him? Will it change your relationship you have established over the years? Being so close may actually make it more difficult for him to share how he really feels."

"Daddy, thank you so much for sharing your wisdom of the man's mind…." Jill hugged her father and they both laughed. "…and thanks for the ice cream, it makes it all go down well."

<u>Chapter Eleven</u>

Courtney continued to hold Marcie and to get as much information as possible from her. Marcie repeated what she had told the paramedic. she didn't actually know what had happened.

Courtney asked Marcie "Is there someone you can call? Your Dad? Are you parents married?"

Marcie replied, "Yes she is married." Courtney suggested, "Would you like to call your father or do you want me to? Marcie rose up and looked at Courtney shrieking an emphatic "NO! YOU

CALL! ...no, please will you call." Courtney recognized the fear in Marcie's voice and eyes. If she was in doubt before she was sure now. Mrs. Selma Taylor was beaten by her husband, and this secret abuse had been going on for quite some time. Courtney knew she had to get someone from the Women's Abuse Center in place quickly. She needed to learn if Marcie could stay somewhere else tonight and not go back home. Courtney agreed, "No problem Marcie, I will place the call. What's the number?" As Marcie gave Courtney the number, j alarms started going off in the emergency room. Someone was flat lining; Courtney got up to leave the room. She said, "Marcie you stay right here."

As Courtney moved quickly from the room, Marcie thought that it might be her mother who was in distress. Marcie had no indication where they had taken her mother, or the extent of her injuries. Just then Marcie heard someone say "CLEAR, stay with us Mrs. Perry, stay with us." Marcie thought to herself, did she hear what she thought? "Mrs. Perry, Mrs. Perry, can you hear me, CLEAR!" Just then she heard the nurse say,"She is back with us Doctor". Marcie came out of the room; she was well aware that there was more then one Mrs. Perry, but she wanted to make certain. Sure enough, there she laid; Mrs. Perry with tubes and doctors and nurses surrounding her. Marcie cried out "Oh No, this is just too much!"

Chapter Twelve

Henry entered the house after Stephanie, who
retreated to herbedroom and begn to change into
her workout clothes. Henry knew that Stephanie
was really heated now. She often worked out in
the morning only, if she worked out in the evening
or the middle of the day she was working off some
anger. Henry struggled to figure if he should say
something or just let Stephanie cool off. He didn't
want his wife mad at him. Their marriage had
already suffered enough of that. However, if he

didn't say anything he could stay away from expressing his opinion about Shane and Jill. Henry decided that he wouldn't say a word, but just would give Stephanie a hug and kiss to demonstrate his affection and empathy. Henry walked up behind her and wrapped his arms around her waist. Stephanie moved away from Henry and put her ear buds on from her iPod. She before walking out ofthe room. Henry sat on the bed, laid back, and let out a big sigh.

In the doorway of the bedroom, there stood Shane. "Hey Dad, you got a minute…. Well more like a few minutes….uhm to talk?" Henry knew what was coming, "Yes, son what's on your mind?" Shane laid down on the chaise lounge in his parent's master bedroom;this was always his place of rest when he came into their room. Henry and Stephanie's room was more like a suite versus a master bedroom. His and Her chaise lounges were located in the sunken area of their bedroom. A mini bar and fifty-inch flat screen television also occupied this space. Henry went behind the bar and grabbed a bottle of water. "Well it sounds like I will need a nice cold one for this talk." Henry chuckled to lighten the mood. But it didn't work. Shane still appeared to be perplexed. "What's on your mind son?" "Dad, have you ever been afraid to express your inner-self?" Henry's stomach went into knots. Even though he suspected this conversation was coming, now he had to engage in a conversation he didn't want to have; not with Stephanie, and *definitely* not with Shane. "Yes son, I have been afraid to express my inner-self."

There was a little break of silence. Henry answered the question as he took a sip of water. "OK, so are you going to elaborate? How did you get over it, work through it?" asked Shane. Henry decided to get straight to the point by asking the clarifying question. "Shane is this about Jill?" There was more silence and Henry wanted to hear the word "no", but he knew that wasn't going to be the case. Shane threw his head back on the chaise and let out the biggest sigh, "Yes, Yes it is!" Henry sighed himself and said, "So, bottom line son, you like her?" "Dad, it's more than just like. I could marry Jill. I've known her all my life. We get along extremely well. I know her better then she knows herself and she probably knows me better then I know myself. We've always talked about everything. This is the first time I've talked out something I was feeling or what was going on with me, with someone else before Jill. Dad, I've talked to you a lot, but I have always talked it out with Jill first. Dad, I know Jill is my wife." Henry was absolutely flabbergasted and didn't know how to respond. This is much deeper than he thought. He just thought this would be some kind of temporal puppy love. Obviously, this was not the case, Stephanie was righ,t and Henry was going to have to process his feelings sooner than he believed. "Shane, you both have to finish school this fall and then there is college. Your head needs to be focused on your books before thinking about a wife." Shane was a little taken aback by his father's stance. "Dad, you and Mom started seeing each other in your sophomore year of high school through college. I don't understand

85

why you are…" Henry interrupts Shane. "Man, I just want you and Jill to concentrate on your studies, live your life, travel and see the world." Shane felt a slight irritation with his Dad at this point. Not understanding why his Dad appeared to be discouraging him, he decided that his dad might need some reassuring that he did intend to complete his education."Dad, I'm not going to ask her to marry me tomorrow. I plan to finish school. I've narrowed down my college selection to Penn State or Stanford, and you can rest assured that I will finish. You sound as if you don't want me to pursue Jill as a wife? Why is that? Uncle Carl and Aunt Jess, you all get along so well and have known each other forever….why wouldn't you want me to consider Jill?" Henry gulped down his water and weighing how he should respond to his son in a way that was dissimilar to his earlier response to Stephanie. He didn't want to make the same mistake twice in one day. "Son, I'm not discouraging you. I just want you to consider your options..." Shane interrupted, "Dad what options? There is no one else I am remotely interested in. I know Jill is the one. I am trying to understand why you are trying to talk me out of this?" "Shane, I am not trying to talk you out of it. If Jill is the one......uhm she's the one." Shane still perplexed says, "I just thought you would be happy for me, or least......I don't know. This reaction is definitely not what I expected!" Henry shifting in his seat said, "I want you to be happy. I feel that it's my responsibility to give you all sides to consider. Have you thought about how she will respond, especially since you two are so close?

Are you willing to risk your current relationship if you express how you feel and she doesn't feel the same way?" Shane just shook his head in disbelief. He was feeling so disappointed in his Dad. He actually would have expected this reaction from his mom, but not his dad. "Dad, of course I'vethought about it. That is the main reason for my hesitation…but you have made me realize it's worth the risk." As Shane stood up from the chaise, his dad stood up with him and said, "Shane, I love you man and I want you to be happy. Please understand that...no matter what, your happiness is in the fore front of my mind." They hugged and Shane left the room. Henry sat back on the chaise with his head in his hand. He looked up and said, "God…I hear you, I should have taken care of this long ago, but I didn't, so here I am. Give me strength for this, God."

Chapter Thirteen

Jill was sitting in her last class of the day, Advanced Calculus. Jill hadn't been able to concentrate all day. She was hoping to see Shane this morning in English but he had a scheduled doctor's appointment this morning she forgot about. This was the first year that they hadn't had most of their classes together. She wasn't sure if he came to school at all today, but she knew she needed to talk with him and another day couldn't go by. Just then, Mrs. McGregor called on Jill to answer her question. "Ms. Richardson, can you explain this to us?" Jill stuttered, which was not a norm for her at all. "Uhm…." The bell rang just in time. "Everyone enjoy your evening." Mrs. McGregor walked to Jill's desk. "Jill, you okay?" Mrs. McGregor appeared to be concerned and gave no hint of scolding. Jill replied, "Mrs. McGregor, I'm okay; just a little distracted today, but I will be back to myself tomorrow." "Okay, I look forward to having you back, have a good evening." Jill gathered her things, and off to her locker she went. She was hoping that she would see Shane; his locker was across from hers. Jill didn't want to call Shane; she wanted to talk to him face to face. Jill scurried out of Mrs. McGregor's class, passed a couple of her classmates and exchanged evening farewells. Jill ran down the flight of steps, desperately not wanting to miss Shane, she came through the doors of the junior hallway and there stood Shane, by her locker. Jill was relieved and she felt something that she had never felt before when she saw Shane standing leaning with his right leg crossed over the other and his hands in his pockets. She couldn't believe that she was feeling a sense of butterflies in her stomach. She felt nervous and her palms became sweaty at the sight of him.. What was going on? She was actually feeling this way about her best friend. She rubbed her hands together, and then on her pants. Shane looked up and their eyes met. Shane threw up his hand and Jill replied with a hand wave. Jill walked

up to Shane and he said, "Hello Jill." Jill replied

with a smile. "Hi Shane, we need to talk." Shane

immediately grabbed Jill by both her hands and

said, "I know, and I want to go first and I have to

say this no matter what you have to say. I'm sorry

Jill. I am so sorry for shutting you out. I was

wrong for ignoring you during dinner. It was only

because... I couldn't express myself... more like I

was afraid to express myself. Then, when I finally

did, it was with a kiss, and that shouldn't have

happened, not like that. I totally caught you off

guard. I should have talked to you just like we

have done all these years; about everything. I

apologize, will you accept my apology?" Jill

nodded and says "Yes, I ..." Shane interrupted

her, "I'm finished. Jill, you and I are like brother

and sister. We have been so close ever since we were babies, you know those pictures of us sleeping together in the play pin and how could we forget the video of us swamping bottles back and forth. Our parents gota kick out of watching..." Jill and Shane both laughed. Shane slid down the front of the lockers to sit on the floor. Jill followed, because Shane was holding both of her hands so tightly. "My love for you was building then and has grown over the years. Everyone says we are more like brother and sister than friends. Well, my love for you has definitely surpassed that of a brother. I can't tell you when it happened, it just did. Jill, I love you and I can see myself spending the rest of my life with you, and I would be honored if you would consider dating me to work toward that end." Jill sat there, eyes wide open in shock, but not so much disbelief.

Shane was patient with Jill, he didn't want to force

her or make her feel uncomfortable, so he chimed

back in. "I don't want you to feel pressured to

answer now, we can talk, you can ask me

questions, we can talk some more and you can

think about it, and do that processing thing you

do." Shane laughed and poked Jill in her side,

because he knows she's so ticklish. He hoped that

this would break the ice. Then he spoke again,

"...and if you don't feel this way, its okay. We can

still be friends and I hope you won't feel

uncomfortable, since I've expressed how I

feel....okay? Now I am finished....I think." Shane

chuckled and pulled Jill's hands up to his lips and

kissed each hand. He not only wanted to break the

ice, but he also wanted to soften the blow, in case

Jill said she just wanted to be friends. Jill looked at Shane almost as if she wasn't sure what to say. Shane continued to give her time to respond until he couldn't take it any more. "Oh Jill, you are killing me now, please say something!" Jill laughed and finally said, "Shane I guess I don't have to tell you how shocked I am. You are right this has really caught me off guard. Everyone around me seemed to see what I was missing. It wasn't until I talked with my father yesterday that I could finally see…" Shane's eyes were big, "You told Uncle Carl, Oh God!" "No, I didn't tell him everything…I was having a hard enough time talking to him about you, let alone telling him my first and only kiss was the reason I was in a state of shock…." Shane appeared to be relieved; he knew that his conversation with his Dad didn't go well, so he was really concerned that the two of them would talk. "…Daddy helped me see what every one else was seeing. I just thought you were being the caring, kind-hearted, thoughtful, considerate, adorable, selfless, loving, adorable, irresistible…." Just then, Shane and Jill found themselves embraced and lips interlocked. Shane pulled away from Jill, to see her expression. She smiled at Shane and Shane returned the favor. "So….I didn't let you finish, but does this mean you are willing to work toward the end of spending your life with me?" Jill smiled and said, "Well, don't you think that you need to talk with my parents, before we make that decision?" Shane replied confidently, "First, I need to make sure that's what you want. Conversation with Uncle Carl and Aunt Jess, *that's easy!*" Shane leaned forward and kissed Jill on her forehead. Shane and Jill continued to look at each other with the goo golly eyes of love.

Over the P.A. the announcement is made *"Chess Club has been canceled for today; and would Shane McFinley and Jill Richardson please report to the main office?"* Shane and Jill looked at each other. "What did you do?"Shane asked. Jill responded, "I was going to ask you the same thing…it's because you kissed me for the second time and someone has told our parents." Shane grabbed Jill's hand and said, "Jill, that is not funny and you would probably pass out on me if we get around here and our parents are standing there." Jill stopped laughing and said, "You know what? You're right, that isn't funny!" Jill didn't drop any books off at her locker. She and Shane, hand in hand, started walking to the main office. Jill and Shane continued to discuss the next level of their relationship. They entered the main hallway, laughingand enjoying each other's company, as they had in days past, but it's obvious by the newly expressed laughter, that love is the center of the atmosphere. Shane and Jill's interlocked hands further confirmed this observation. Shane's laughter stops when he noticed that both his mom and Aunt Jess were standing outside of the office. Shane didn't want to spook Jill and release her hand, but he didn't want her to be uncomfortable with this outward display of affection. Shane tightened his grip on Jill's hand and said "Jill, you are not going to believe this…" Jill looked at Shane and noticed he was staring straight ahead. Jill turned to see what had captured Shane's attention, and then Jill felt as if her legs were going to give out from under her. Shane felt Jill tense up, But, he refused to let go of her hand. He held tighter and whispered "…its okay. Hey Mom, Aunt Jess what are you two doing here?"

Stephanie and Jessica were standing outside of the main office, both of them looking very troubled. However, Stephanie and Jessica looked at each other, because they both noticed the difference between Jill and Shane. The hand holding was just an outward confirmation. Jessica said to Stephanie, "This is not the time for you to tell me, I told you so."

Chapter Fourteen

Jill and Shane greeted their mothers and Jill said, "Mom, what are you doing here?" "Yeah, Mom, what's up?" asked Shane. Jessica said, "We thought it would be best to come and pick you up." Jill looked at her mom and said, "Mom what's wrong? Please what's wrong? Is it Dad? Uncle Carl?" "No dear, it's Mrs. Perry. She was rushed to North General last night; it's believed that she had a stroke. Jill began to cry "What?!" Shane tried to stay strong for Jill, but he was unable to hold back the tears. He asked, "Is she going to be OK?" . Shane's mom replied, "Shane, right now the doctors are not sure." Jessica moved to put her arms around Jill to console her, but Jill lets out a loud cry "Oh God, not Granny P!" before falling into Shane's arms. Shane cuddled and held Jill as the tears poured from his eyes. "OK, let's go then, let's get there to Granny," said Shane. Jessica and Stephanie looked at each other. There are two situations now, Granny P, and the budding relationship of Shane and Jill.

Chapter Fifteen

Carl returned to his office with his assistant
walking behind him giving him updates and
announcing the completion of assignments since
he has been in meetings all day. His assistant had
set appointments for the week, which included
luncheons with colleagues and weekly flower
orders to his wife. "Tonya, thank you for the
updates, that will be all, please close the door
behind you" said Carl. Carl sat at his desk checks
his emails and listens to his personal voicemails.

He decided not to listen to all of the messages, scanning and deleting them, hoping to get home a little early. After four messages, the next voice caused him to stop reading his email. A small lump immediately formed in his throat. "Hello Carl, it was good to see you yesterday, I hope…" Just then his phone rang, which startled Carl. Trying to gain his composure, he activated the speakerphone. "Yes?" Tonya's voice came over the speaker phone. "Mr. McFinley is here to see you." "OK, send him in," said Carl.

Henry walked in. "Hey what's up man? I emailed you and I didn't hear back from you. I thought I would stop by. Want to hit the greens?" Carl sat back in his chair staring into space, as if he had

seen a ghost. "Carl what's up man, you OK?"
Henry sat down in Carl's high back Italian leather
chair. "Man, I just got in the office and I was
checking my voicemail. You're not going to guess
had left me a message? *Beverly! Man can you*
believe that woman?!" Carl shifted, in his chair.
"Alright Carl, m-a—a-n you have got to put a stop
to this. Has she been contacting you, or was
Sunday the first time?" Henry stood up and gazed
out of his sixteenth floor corner office as he spoke,
"Carl, Sunday was the first time in forever! I
haven't seen this woman in five years, honestly!"
"Man, I don't have to tell you how Jessica would
respond. You've got to tell her…" "Henry
man…I don't know if this is a good time." "Why,
what's up? You don't want her to find out that
Beverly has been contacting you. You and Beverly

had an affair. And do I need to remind you that the affair was for five years. It took a long time for Jessica to build her trust in you." "I know, but Henry I'm not her favorite person right now, and bringing this up is not going to help the situation." "Well man, we are so connected it appears we find ourselves in the same situations all the time, Stephanie is upset with me right now too. Why is Jessica mad at you?" "Well, did Stephanie talk to you about why she and Jessica had their uncharacteristic spat? In that moment, Henry wished he hadn't stopped by Carl's office, but he played it cool. "Aw man, yeah Stephanie is not happy with me about it at all. I tried to make her see Jessica's point of view." Carl was a little taken back, "Really, I tried to get Jessica to see Stephanie's point of view. Henry, we should have seen this coming. I consider it an honor for Shane to be interested in Jill. What more could I ask for? Jessica didn't see it that way, and I have to tell you, I'm surprised." Henry, felt a little more relaxedat this point, "Carl, I told Stephanie, Jessica was probably thinking about Jill's schooling, maintaining her concentration and not getting caught up in a relationship at this young age." Carl walked toward Henry. "You are really surprising me. You and my wife actually sound alike. Are you saying that *you* don't want Shane and Jill to see each other? And, if you don't, I have to ask you, why? We've known each other for years. We're the best of friends, like brothers man. What more could we ask for?" Henry knew that his next statement was going to be crucial. He already had his wife upset with him, and his son disappointed. Henry knew ver well that he couldn't afford to have his best friend not speaking to him. "Man, like I told Stephanie and Shane, I am not saying that…" Carl interrupted, "You told Shane? Shane has talked to you about this?" Henry could have kicked himself. He should have never said Shane's name. Henry didn't want to lie to Carl, he just wanted to approach this issue with kid gloves. He already asked God for help; Henry knew this was God telling him to deal with this. Just then the phone rang, "Carl answered, "What?! OK, we're on the way. Henry is here in the office with me." Henry moved to the edge of the chair. "*What's up now!?*" Carl hung up the phone and looked up at Henry. "That was Jessica, it's Granny P she's in the hospital, and it's not looking good. She and

107

Stephanie have the kids and they're on their way

to North General."

Chapter Sixteen

Marcie sat by her mother's bedside. There are tubes and monitors all around her mother.. Broken blood vessels could be seen in her mother's face, her left eye was swollen five times its size. A bandage covered the right eye. Selma's lips look swollen, purple and cut in two different places. One leg is broken; her arms are bruised and discolored. Marcie looked at her mother and thought, *"how did we arrive at this point?"*

Courtney knocked on the door and entered. Marcie jumped. She is so on edge. She didn't sleep last night, she was expecting her father to show up at any moment. She's terrified, wondering what his presence will bring.

"Hello Marcie, I didn't mean to scare you. I haven't been able to reach your father." Marcie breathed a little relief. "Thank you Courtney…uhm…did you leave a message when you called?" "Yes, I introduced myself and asked him to call me back. I gave my direct line, it will forward to this phone if I don't answer." Courtney pulled out the standard hospital wireless phone. The phone rang. Marcie jumped out of her seat and moved toward the window. Courtney knew that now is the time for her to sit and have a serious discussion with Marcie. "Hello, this is Courtney. Yes, that's fine, thank you." Courtney walked toward Marcie. "Marcie, what do you say we grab some breakfast." "I am not very hungry..." "I know you haven't eaten, because I ordered you a tray that you didn't accept. Marcie you need to eat something." Marcie responded, "I want to be here when my mom wakes up." Courtney assured her, "We won't be long."

Marcie and Courtney head down to the cafeteria. On the way, Courtney tries to make small talk with Marcie; asking her about school and any extra-curricular activities she may be involved in. Marcie wanted to talk. In fact, she really *needed* to talk to someone, but she was so afraid of her father that she didn't know if she could trust

Courtney. They arrived at the cafeteria. Marcie got
a bottle of water. Courtney picked up a salad for
her and Marcie. "Courtney, that's very nice of
you, but I really don't feel like eating." "Well, if
you don't want to eat it now, you can eat it later."
Courtney selected a table that was secluded from
other customers in the cafeteria. "Marcie, I know
that you don't know me, and asking you to trust
that you can talk to me, sounds easier said than
done.. I told you last night, I know that your
mother's injuries were not self inflicted. I grew up
very much like you, and I remember coming into
the emergency room with my mother the same
way you did last night. I was silent for so many
years and when I had the opportunity to get away
and help my mother…I didn't because I was too
afraid. The difference between you and me, is that

112

my mother didn't make it that night. That was my
third trip with my mother to the emergency room.
The third time was the clincher that ended her life.
I continued to live in hell for the next four years
with my father; all because I wouldn't open my
mouth." Marcie just stared at Courtney with tears
streaming down her face. Courtney's phone rang
again.. "Marcie, your mother is conscious."

Chapter Seventeen

Carl and Henry decided to take one car to the
hospital. Carl was the designated driver and Henry
dropped his car off at home. Carl wanted to
continue their conversation concerning their
children dating. "Henry, you know we have to
finish talking about this issue regarding Jill and
Shane." "Man, look, I already have Stephanie and
Shane upset with me." "Yeah, so let me get this
straight. You mean to tell me that you knew about
this?" "No, Carl, this was all sprung on me

yesterday. Stephanie was grinding me about it after dinner. She didn't believe that I couldn't see that Shane was interested in Jill. Honestly man, I didn't notice. It could have been because I didn't want to." "Really!? I asked Jessica the same thing; she acted as if she did not notice. If *I noticed*, I know Jessica noticed.o, I'mm going to ask you right out. Why are you not for this relationship?" "Carl, I am not saying that, I just thought that Jill and Shane should concentrate on completing their studies before committing to a relationship. You know, Shane brought up that I have been involved with his mother since our sophomore year of high school, so that didn't fly very well. There are two things I know, I want Jill and Shane to be happy and I don't want our relationship to be in jeopardy." Carl stopped at the light at the entrance of the hospital and looked at Henry. "Man, we've

been friends for years. I'm hoping that this won't

jeopardize our friendship."

Chapter Eighteen

Marcie and Courtney were in the elevator when it stopped at the main floor. When the door opened Marcie had no where to hide, no where to turn. What had been held as a secret for so long was finally coming out. Her mind raced trying to determine what would happen next. Marcie stood frozen, as she heard rounds of "Hello Marcie." Shane and Jill walked into the elevator first with Jessica and Stephanie behind them. Jessica managed to get close to Marcie to see if she was okay. "Hi, Marcie, what are you doing here? Where is your mom? Are you here to see Mrs. Perry?" Jessica unleashed a series of questions that left Marcie even more paralyzed. Stephanie placed her hand on Marcie's shoulder. "Marcie, are you okay?" Jessica didn't want to presume, but she was pretty sure that Marcie wasn't there to see Mrs. Perry. She was hoping that would be the case, but considering the behavior of the family over the last two years, she knew the worst. "Where is your mom, Marcie?" Marcie finally dropped her head. The elevator door opened, Shane said, "Mom, this is the floor." Jessica looked at Stephanie and they both knew. Stephanie nodded at Jessica giving her approval of her unspoken next move. Jessica thought that Shane was pretty stable, but Stephanie needed to be there for Jill. "You all go ahead, I am going to stay with Marcie and I will be down later." Stephanie said, "Come on, let's see Mrs. Perry kids. Marcie, we'll come up and check on you later as well." The evaluator door closed. Courtney was happy to have the reinforcements, even though she had a strong sense that these unexpected visitors wouldn't open Marcie up either. Courtney wanted to introduce herself, but she thought this might be the opportunity for Marcie to open up. Jessica put her arm around Marcie. "Marcie what's going on, talk to me. Is it your mom?" Marcie broke down in tears in Jessica's arm. Courtney came around the two of them and introduced herself. "Hi, I'm Courtney, a lead nurse here at North General. I was on duty when Marcie and her mother came in. Are you a relative?" Jessica replied, "No, my name is Jessica Richardson. Marcie and I are members of the same church. What happened? Is it Selma? Is she OK?" Marcie cried louder in Jessica's arm when she asked that question.. "Marcie, can you tell Mrs. Richardson what happened?" Jessica looked at Courtney and Courtney hoped that Mrs. Richardson would go along with what she was trying to do. "Marcie looked up at Courtney crying and yelling, "I HAVE ALREADY TOLD YOU, I DON'T KNOW…I FOUND HER COVERED IN BLOOD!!!" Jessica held Marcie tighter. The elevator door opened and Courtney took Marcie and Mrs. Richardson into a consultation room. "Mrs. Richardson..." Courtney begins. "Mrs. Richardson is not necessary. Call me Jessica, please." Courtney begins again,

"Jessica, I have been trying to reach Mrs. Taylor's husband, but he has yet to return my call. Do you know how we can contact him?" Jessica replied, "I don't. Please, can you tell me what happened to Selma and how she is?" "I'm not actually sure what occurred. I was hoping Marcie could share that with me, but what I do know is that Marcie heard her mother screaming and she found her outside of their home covered in blood. I also know and have shared with Marcie that theses wounds are not self inflicted..." Jessica, still holding Marcie, realized that her suspicions might have been true after all. Courtney continued, "...Jessica, I must warn you, when you go in to see her, you should expect the worse, that way you won't be taken by surprise. Mrs. Taylor has sustained quite a number of injuries. She is fortunate to be alive. Marcie and I e were coming back to the room because I just received a call that Mrs. Taylor has regained consciousness. "Thank you for preparing me and sharing with me what you know. I would like to go see Mrs. Taylor now," said Jessica.

Courtney, Marcie and Jessica walked down to Selma's room. Marcie entereds through the door first. Her mother turned and saw Marcie. Marcie ran to her mother's bedside, still in tears. Selma began to cry.

She painfully moves her arm to touch Marcie. You could see the tears building up around Selma's eye. Marcie was so happy to see her mother awake and responsive that she didn't even notice the man standing on the opposite side of the bed.

Courtney had immediately noticed the man and was just beginning to ask the gentleman if he was Mr. Taylor, when Jessica said, "Hello Mark." "Hello Jessica, how are you?" Courtney said, "Are you Mr. Taylor?" Mark extended his hand and replied, "Oh no, I'm Mark Swindoll. I attend church with the Taylor and Richardson families. I'l let you have your visit now; I just came from visiting with Mrs. Perry." Jessica said, "I was on my way there when I saw Marcie." Mark moved closer to Selma's bed, told her to take care, and gave his farewells. Jessica was very surprised to see Mark there at the hospital. Jessica and Stephanie were on the Pastoral Care team, and that team usually wass made aware of hospitalizations before for the rest of the church body.

Marcie was still crying by her mother's side.

Courtney moved a chair to Selma's bedside so so could sit down. "Hello, Mrs. Taylor, my name is Courtney Morgan. I am the lead emergency nurse. I was on duty when you and Marcie arrived at North General. You have a very lovely daughter." Selma tried to smile through her tear stricken face. Courtney continued, "Mrs. Taylor, I have tried repeatedly to contact your husband. I will inform him about your condition the moment he calls…" Selma didn't appear to respond about her husband's lack of response. "…Mrs. Taylor, can you tell me what happened?" Selma just began to cry and shaking her head from left right. She slowly opened her mouth, but she could not utter any words, despite her trying. Courtney replied, "Mrs. Taylor, we can talk about this later. Has

124

anyone come in and discussed your injuries? Selma nodded her head yes. Courtney thought it would be best if she left Jessica alone with Marcie and Selma. Maybe Jessica could get further with the two of them. Courtney looked at Jessica and told her she was going to check in at the nurses' station and would return.

Jessica moved closer to Selma's bed. Jessica knew this was a very sensitive moment and this could go south very quickly if not handled correctly. "Selma, I know you can't talk well...and moving your head doesn't appear to be the best for you at this point. So, if you could blink once for no, and twice for yes..." Marcie looked up and Selma blinked twice. "...okay, were you beaten?" Selma blinked twice. Jessica was breathing deeply.

"Okay, did Cal do this?" Just then, Cal Taylor busted through the door. Marcie clinched the hand railing on her mother's bed, every monitor; light and buzzer connected to Selma lit up and rang throughout the hospital room.

Chapter Nineteen

Stephanie, Shane and Jill walked into Mrs. Perry's room. Mrs. Perry had an oxygen tube and monitors on the side of her bed. Jill and Shane both ran to her bedside. Jill and Shane grabbed her hand, which appeared withered due to the stroke.

Granny P opened her eyes and struggled to speak, "My babies, Granny P's babies!" Jill and Shane both had tears streaming down their faces, but Jill couldn't hold back her tears and she cried in Shane's arms as they both continued to hold Granny P's hand. Stephanie came up behind Shane and Jill and held them both. Granny continued to struggle to speak, her speech was a whisper, but she made herself heard. "NO! NO! NO! NO tears... no tears babies, no tears. My God is a faithful God!" After witnessing Granny P's resolve to be a strong witness, even in this condition, Stephanie also broke into tears. They all held on to each other.

Carl and Henry finally arrive. They walked into the room. Henry went to Stephanie's side; Carl went around the other side of the bed and kissed

Granny P on her forehead. Henry then followed.

Carl said, "Where is Jessica?" Stephanie replied,

"Selma Taylor is upstairs on the sixth floor.

Jessica went to check on her and Marcie." Carl

and Henry instantly were concerned about Jessica,

since they all had there suspicions about Cal

Taylor. Carl told Henry, "I'm going to go and

check on Jessica." Henry nodded and stayed with

his family and Jill.

Carl walked down the hallway as fast as he could

without making a disturbance on the tile floor.

Carl pushed the "up" button of the elevator and it

seemed that the elevators were taking an eternity.

He watched the indicators of the four elevators;

only one elevator appeared to be coming to his

rescue, but it stopped on floor two. Carl continued

to push the elevator button, as if that would make the elevator come faster. Carl couldn't wait any longer. He ran to the stairwell and sprinted up four flights of steps to get to Jessica. Carl entered through the six-floor stairwell. Breathing heavily, he walked to the nurses' station and asked, "What is Selma Taylor's room?" the nurse replied, "Room 624, but sir this may not be the best…." As he ran down the hall, Carl could hear alarms and see people running. He could hear a loud man's voice, but couldn't recognize if it was Cal's or not. He was hoping it wasn't Selma's room, but to his dismay it was. .

When Carl arrived at the room, He saw Jessica in one corner with Marcie standing behind her. Cal was ranting, "*I CAN'T BELIEVE THAT YOU'RE*

IN A PRIVATE ROOM! DO YOU KNOW HOW

MUCH THIS COSTS?" he was obviously drunk

and was staggering.. Selma's monitors were

ringing and pinging out of control. Her blood

pressure was rising like the morning ocean tide.

Nurses and orderlies were trying to get Cal out of

the room, but he was insisting that he stay in the

room with his family. He made it clear that since it

was the room that he was going to be paying for,

he would leave it only when he was good and

ready to do so.Marcie was crying and shaking

hysterically. "I'mm paying for this room, this is

my wife, and I am not going anywhere. " Cal

slurred.. Another nurse came in behind Carl, it

was Courtney, "Oh my God, is this Mr. Taylor?"

Carl replied, "Yes, it is!" All of this was

happening so fast. Carl moved into the room and

took Cal by his arm. "Come on Cal, its Carl Richardson. Let's go out, so they can work on Selma." Cal was so drunk he didn't recognize Carl. "Who are you? So *you* are the one messing around with my wife!!" "What! Naw man, it's Carl Richardson from church. You are upsetting your wife being in here, let's go and let's go now!" Cal continued to be difficult and loads of nonsense continued to spew from his mouth. Just then, the cavalry arrived. Henry was there, as always, to back Carl up. "You heard him Cal, let's go. Carl and Henry both were able to get Cal out of the room, he went reluctantly, but he was no match for the former Miami U linebackers.

Chapter Twenty

Richardson and Associates was just about to close

their office, when the receptionist looked up, "Oh

my, how are you, I haven't seen you in so long?

What have you been up to?" Beverly Martinez

replied, "I'veve been keeping out of trouble. Is

Carl in his office?" The receptionist replied, "No

he isn't, but if you'd like to leave a message, I'lll

be sure to give it to him. "I just have something I

want to place in his office. Is his assistant, Tonya,

still here, or has she gone for the day?" The

receptionist responded, "I believe she's still here, let me call her..." Beverly began to walk toward the back, "Oh that won't be necessary, I will only be a minute..." "Beverly, you know that I can't let you go back, Beverly...stop." Beverly continued to walk back, toward the offices. What Beverly was not aware of, was the fact that additional security measures had been put in place after her departure with Richardson and Associates. The glass doors to the offices were now locked, and Beverly couldn't return to the lobby because the main door locked behind her. The receptionist immediately followed protocol by calling security and making the emergency page for any persons still in the office. Tonya heard the page. She and one other paralegal were still in the office. The paralegal ran to Tonya's desk with all of her belongings in hand. "Are you ready to get out of here?" Tonya replied, we can lock ourselves in an office, but we can't leave, because the intruder may be in the stairwell. Follow me." Tonya grabbed her belongings and they locked themselves in Carl Richardson's office.

Security arrived and the receptionist told them where Beverly was. The security officers opened the door, and there Beverly stood with her arms folded, obviously very perturbed, and now embarrassed by the whole situation. However, one thing Beverly was good at was manipulation. "Hello gentleman, have you arrived to escort me back to the offices?" "No ma'am, we will be escorting you off the premises." Beverly began to work her charm. "Oh, there must be some type of misunderstanding. I just wanted to leave a gift for my boyfriend. I don't know why you were called." "Ma'am, we will be glad to take your package, but you must leave, NOW!." "Well, I know you both are just doing your job. I will comply with your wishes" Beverly relentsAs Beverly exited being escorted by the guards, she looked at the receptionist, cutting her eyes. As she leaves, she flashes a sarcastic smile and said,, "Well, this has been an enlightening visit. Enjoy your evening."

The security guards walked Beverly out. The receptionist announced an "All Clear" page. Tonya and the other paralegal exited from Carl's office and proceeded to the main lobby. Tonya, wanting to know what all happened, asked "What in the world is going on, who was that?" The receptionist sat down in her chair in relief, "Girl, it was Beverly Martinez; she wanted to put something on Mr. Richardson's desk. I told her that I would check to see if you were still in the office and that she couldn't go back to the office without an escort". Tonya horrified said, "Well, you did the right thing! She didn't leave the package in Mr. Richardson's office, did she?" "No, the security guards followed protocol and took the package," said the receptionist. " I don't know about *you* ladies, but I am ready to go! This paralegal has had enough today at Richardson and Associates." The women waited for the receptionist to get her things to exit the building together. "As a precaution I think that we should stay together, I will drive everyone to their car,"

said Tonya. They all agreed that would be best.

Chapter Twenty-One

Calvin Taylor was being strong armed out of his wife's room. All the while, Calvin Taylor was embarrassing and belligerent. Carl and Henry were taking Calvin to the waiting room right next to the elevators, but just before arriving Calvin passed out. "Oh Jesus, you have got to be kidding….all this and now he passes out on us?!" said Henry. Carl replied, "We should be grateful; at least we won't have to knock him out.. Can you believe all that Selma has been dealing with?"

"There'ss nothing that surprises me anymore. I hate that his life has resorted to this. This confirms that money doesn't make the man!" "So true! Thanks for coming to my rescue; your timing was impeccable Mr. McFinley" "Mr. Richardson the pleasure was mine!" They both laugh slapping each other's hand with their familiar hand shake "Henry man, we've been through a lot together. I would have to say this is a first." Henry muses, "No, this is not the first. Remember, we had to carry Bruce Jefferson back to the dorm, so the coach wouldn't catch him passed out in the campus fountain." "Oh yeah, I forgot about that!" "We have some stories don't we?" said Henry. "Yes, we do and it appears that we may be telling our grandchildren together." "OK Carl, don't start with that. Shane and Jill are not even married yet!"

139

"Man, I don't know what your problem is, but you better work it out and work it out fast! I'm going to check on Jessica," said Carl. Henry got up behind Carl; "OK, let's go!" "Who's going to stay here with Calvin?" asked Carl. "You're not leaving *me* here with this grown man that can't hold his liquor," said Henry.

Carl and Henry arrive back in Selma's room, it's a lot calmer but the emotions are still high considering the recent drama. The nurses have gotten Selma's blood pressure down and she appears to have stabilized with the appropriate medication. The nurses asked that we leave and allow Selma to get some rest.. Marcie is clinging to her mother's bed. "I'm not leaving; I can't leave" Marcie said through her tears. Courtney stepped up and asked Marcie to come with her just to get some fresh air. Marcie refused and said "What if my father comes back?" Courtney replied, "I've called security and they are going to escort your father out of the hospital." Marcie still refused to leave. "Marcie you can't stay here all night, you can come home with Mr. Richardson and I. Carl, will that be alright with you?" "Absolutely, I'm sure Jill will welcome the company." Marcie, although apprehensive about leaving her mother's bedside, finally agreed."I really appreciate you all. I don't know what I would have done if you weren't here. I just don't want to leave my mom right now knowing…" Marcie just broke down. Jessica continued to try to console Marcie. "…please Courtney let me stay a little while longer. Courtney understood

Marcie's apprehension. "Mrs. Richardson, if it's okay, can you come back when visiting hours are over?" With a smile, Jessica nodded. . "Of course Marcie, let's consider it a plan!" Jessica gives her one more hug before departing.

Courtney, Jessica, Carl and Henry all walk out of the room. Courtney closes the door behind them. Jessica expressed her outrage about Cal's display of anger earlier."What can be done to ensure that lunatic doesn't get back in to Selma's room?!"?" Courtney assured Jessica that she had taken the proper steps to contact security; if the situation arises, security assured her that the ywould immediately contact the police and properly escort Mr. Taylor out of the hospital. Courtney asked, "Where'ss Mr. Taylor?" "He's passed out in the waiting area near the elevator." Henry replied.

Courtney was relieved, "Good, that's where I told the security guards to go." Jessica asked "What other protection can be given?" Carl stepped in, because now, this legal aspect was hisexpertise. "Honey, unless Selma files for a restraining order, she and Marcie will be at risk when she leaves the hospital." Courtney chimed in, "With Mrs. Taylor's injuries, she won't be leaving for some time. Maybe that will give her the necessary time to think things over." Jessica hugged Courtney and thanked her for all of her help. Courtney replied, "It is my pleasure to assist Selma in any way that I can. I've been in Marcie's shoes. My father beat my mother literally to death. I was too afraid to say anything ,and my mother lost her life because of it. So, I'm very much in touch with Marcie's state of mind; that is her fear and uneasiness of leaving her mother's side. As the child of an abused parent, you feel responsible and helpless, all at the same time;wishing that you could just take the necessary step to do something. And if the father is beating or being abusive in any way towards the child, that addsanother layer to the onion." Carl asked,, "Do you think Cal is beating Marcie? Did she show any physical evidence of abuse?" Courtney was unable to say for sure. "Mr. Richardson, I didn't do a complete examination on Marcie. I do know that she didn't appear to have sustained any injuries when she came in yesterday." Henry was sickened, "What man could physically abuse his family?" Courtney turned and responded Henry. "You would be surprised."

Chapter Twenty-two

Carl, Jessica and Henry arrived back at Mrs.

Perry's room. Jessica looked at Stephanie, who

had remained with Mrs. Perry, and asked, "How is

shedoing?" "Stable for now.She'ss in and out.

She's aware enough of what is going on to tell us

to stop crying, and that God is faithful." "Well,

she's doing pretty well considering that *she's* the

one comforting *us*. ," said Henry. That brought a

little chuckle to everyone in the room.

Stephanie asked, "How's everything with Selma, she okay?" Jessica threw up her hands and said, "Drama Girl! Just Drama! My suspicions were right. Maybe we should go down to the cafeteria to have a little dinner, and we can discuss all that's happened today." Everyone agreed, with the exception of Shane and Jill. They aske if they could stay behind. Carl responded, "Sure, here's some mone, in case you come down later." Carl pulled out his normal wad of pocket money and handed them each twenty dollars. Shane and Jill were both thankful.

Just as Shane and Jill started out the door,, Granny P roused,, "Come here you two." Taken by surprise and quite pleased, they hasten to Granny P's bedside. "Come closer, I want to make sure

147

you can hear me," said Granny P. "You two promise me that you will always follow God. Put Him first and lean not to your own understanding; acknowledge Him in all your ways…" Jill gazed into Granny's eyes while holding her hand, "Granny, I will. But, don't you leave us. I want you to be around to see us do just that!" Shane chimed in with his arm around Jill's waist "Yeah Granny P., we don't need you leaving anytime soon." "Oh children, I can't be with you always, but while I'm still here, let's talk about your relationship that is noticeably shifting." Shane proudly confirmed Granny P's observation. stated "Granny, you're right. Jill and I are an item, and I want this young lady to be my wife!" Shane begins to act silly, making up a song about Jill being his wife, and dancing with her in the middle of the floor. Granny chuckled, but got a little choked, and started coughing. Jill and Shane helped lift her from her lying position, so Jill could pat her back, hoping that would help. Thank you babies, I'm okay." Jill was relieved. "See Shane you got Granny all worked up!" Granny leaned back and said, "That was without a doubt worth the work up!" Granny threw up the peace sign. They all laughed.

Granny, there's just this little matter. Shane has to talk with my parents about us. After that, it'll be official. ." Jill excused herself to use the restroom.

"Well Shane, that should be easy for you or are you concerned?" "Not really, Granny…but I was

surprised by a conversation I had with my Dad
recently. When I went to him for advice
concerning Jill, I received a totally different vibe
from him than I expected. I expected that my
mom would try to talk me out of marriage, by
using the old *"concentrate on school"* adage. But
it was Dad, that really took me off guard." Before
Granny could respond Jill was back in the room.
Shane changed the subject to give Granny the clue
that he hadn't discussed this issue with Jill.

Granny held her hand up for Jill and Shane to
take. "Take my hand." . Granny began to pray
for Shane and Jill. She gave her blessing for their
relationship, and prayed that the decision that they
had made would result in a strong bond that would
bring Glory to God. Just as she ended her rousing

prayer, the alarm on Granny P's monitor went off. The nurses quickly entered Granny P's room. rooJill and Shane overheard the nurse say, "She's coding" One of the nurses rushed out of the room, while the other nurse worked on Granny P. *"Code Blue! ...Room 502...Code Blue!... Room 502"* echoed throughout the hospital. . As hane and Jill heard the announcement, they both cried out, "Granny P....!!!"

Chapter Twenty-three

After going through the array of food offerings in the cafeteria line, the Richardsons and McFinleys sat down to discuss the status of Selma and Marcie Taylor.

Jessica was still astonished by Cal Taylor's behavior. "My feeling concerning Cal and Selma was right. Cal beat Selma within inches of her life. Marcie is devastated and I don't know how much more she can take. I still can't believe that Cal came in there drunk, ranting and raving. Carl and

Henry arrived just in time." "How is Marcie doing," askedStephanie. "You can imagine…" Carl chimed in "Marcie's not doing well, at all. The poor girl cried in Jessica's arms the whole time. I feel bad for her. Courtney mentioned that she didn't have any injuries. I just wonder if he has beaten Marcie too." Stephanie said, "Who's Courtney?" Henry replied, "Courtney is the lead nurse that was on duty when Marcie and Selma came in last night. Cal needs to have a good old fashion beat down! I know that is not the Godly response…" Stephanie agrees, "No it's not, we have to extend mercy, just as mercy has been extended to each of us."

Jessica shook her head and started to cry, "My heart just goes out to that girl…." Carl comforted

Jessica putting his arm around her shoulders and kissing her head. "Come on babe, it's going to be okay. We'rere going to help any way we can." "I just hope Selma allows us to help her and Marcie through this. Stephanie, what do you suggest...Doctor?" "Well, you know I have seen many cases like this. Selma has to be willing; this is the first time that I am aware of that Selma has been in the hospital. What is the extent of her injuries?" Carl, Henry and Jessica all replied with sighs and words of disgust. Henry said, "Her eye is swollen shut, and that is one eye; the other eye, has a patch on it. Her face and arms are all severely bruised. Her leg is broken and that's what we can see from the outside." Jessica continued to give the update. "Stephanie, it's absolutely horrible...Selma looks bad. Jessica can tell you

154

that Cal came in there in adrunken stupor, shouting foolishness and profanity, every alarm and monitor in her room began to sound. It was just atrocious! Jessica talked Marcie into coming home with us for the night." "Honey, we have to make sure we tell Jill. This has been a rough one for her today; finding out about Granny being hospitalized"Jessica acknowledged Carl's statement with a nod. Everyone was picking over their food when Shane quickly entered the cafeteria. As he came toward the table everyone could see that he had been crying. What's wrong son?, asked Henry. I need to take Jill home. . Granny P flat lined just after praying for Jill and me.. Jill lost it. Thank God they were able to revive Granny. They are requesting that Granny be allowed time torest. I'd like to borrow the car

155

to take Jill home. I was able to finally convince Jill that we needed to leave and let Granny rest.." Henry handed over his keys to Shane, "Son, here are my keys. Carl…Jessica is it okay if you take us home," asked Stephanie. "Absolutely, no problem," said Carl. Shane expressed his thanks and gave his hugs and kisses good bye.

Carl watched Shane as he gave his good byes and stared at him leaving the cafeteria with the same sense of urgency with which he came.. Carl was convinced that Shane would make a perfect mate for Jill and decided he was going to take the risk of making a comment, regardless of Jessica's reaction. "If he can respond this well in crisis, he's going to make a fine son-in-law. I know I won't have to worry about my baby." Jessica cut her eyes and looked at Henry and Stephanie for their responses. Henry didn't even look up from his plate. Stephanie smiled at Carl and said, "Carl, I agree!"

Chapter Twenty-four

Courtney was in the room with Marcie and Selma.

Marcie was still visibly shaken by the events of

the day. Dinner was being served; a tray was

delivered for both Marcie and Selma. Selma was

placed on a soft diet for obvious reasons. Marcie

stood to assist her mother with dinner. "Mommy,

I'llll help feed you.." Selma's eye filled with tears

once again. Mashed potatoes and an

unrecognizable meat item were on the plate, along

with a side of applesauce, apple juice and unsweetened tea. "Mommy, it's not Morton's steak and potatoes, but we can imagine that it is.. Remember the first time you took me there for lunch?" This memory brought a smile to Marcie's face. Courtney was enjoying seeing Marcie reminisce about happier times between her and her mother. However, it wasn't long before Marcie's eyes, were filled again with horrifying tears as she could not forget the days events..

There was a knock at the door, Marcie responded with a jump as she had been doing since arriving at North General. Courtney opened the door to see members of hospital security and two local police officers. Courtney exited the room to talk with the officers in hopes of not making Marcie any more uncomfortable than she already was. The security officer asked, "Is this Selma Taylor's room?" Courtney replied, "Yes, Mr. Taylor has already been removed from the room. He was left in the waiting room; passed out on a couch. One of the officers introduces himself, "Hello, I'm Officer Parker and this is my partner, Officer Burns. We wanted to let you know that we" just left the waiting area, and no one is there." Courtney's heart began to race a little harder. "Oh, no, we have to issue a hospital alert. We also need to have an officer posted at Mrs. Taylor's door. Her husband was drunk and clearly unstable; he had caused such a ruckus on this floor earlier, no telling what he'd do if he was able to get back into Selma's room. Not to mention that his daughter and wife are absolutely terrified." Officer Parker replied, "Ma'am, they don't have anything to worry about. Rest assured, I will be posted for the next five hours. With an additional request from the hospital's administration, we can assign someone for the entire night, or as long as you need." Everyone acknowledged the plan, and Courtney agreed to start the necessary proceedings. She also gave the description of Cal Taylor to issue the hospital alert.

After Courtney finished, she went back into the room with Selma and Marcie. Selma didn't appear to eat much of her food, and Marcie hadn't touch her tray at all. Marcie looked at Courtney, "Did they find my dad?" Courtney didn't hesitate or even attempt to sugar coat the truth. She knew that if she was ever going to gain Marcie's trust, she would always have to be upfront with her. "No, your father was no longer in the waiting room near the elevators when the police arrived. A hospital alert has been issued and a 24-hour guard is being placed outside of your mother's room. We'lll take care of your mother; it will be okay." Marcie looked at Courtney and said, "I feel so ….hopeless. I don't know what to do. Every daughter wants her family to stay together, but I have to ask 'at what cost'. Is this worth it? Courtney, is it worth it?" Courtney understands where Marcie is coming from. "For me Marcie, it wasn't worth it. It cost my mother her life. And even after her death, it caused me four more years of hurt, shame and pain that I didn't need to go through. Marcie you are in a better position than you currently realize. There is still time for you to live a better life. I will do whatever I can to help you," said Courtney. Marcie smiled at Courtney. There appeared to be some glimmer of hope in Marcie's eyes that Courtney had not seen since meeting her.

Chapter Twenty-five

Shane pulled up in front of the hospital. He

jumped out of the car and wentinto the main

lobby. He took Jill by the hand and opened the car

door for her. As Shane and Jill drive away from

the hospital Jill put her hand on Shane's leg and

told him, "Thank you….thank you for taking me

out of there. I didn't want to leave, but it was best

for me to leave." Shane responded to Jill and held

her hand. "You're welcome. Do you want me to

get you something to eat; what about a nice greasy

burger from the Dew Drop Inn? Brother Curtis is probably there cooking them up fresh!" Shane said with a big smile. "No…well I can get a side salad from there; that'ss all I can probably force myself to eat. Shane, do you think Granny P will make it?" He quickly responded, "I'm speaking that to be! Power of life and death is in my tongue, so I'm choosing to speak life concerning Granny P." "That's good. Thanks for the Word; it will keep you… every time if you let it!" said Jill.

Shane walked in the Dew Drop Inn and ordered their food. Upon his return, he asked Jill, "Would you like to go to my house and sit out by the pool and eat?" "That sounds good," Jill responded.. Shane held Jill's hand while riding to his home. He pulled into the circular drive, grabbed the food and moved to the other side of the car to let Jill out. Shane entered the code for the front door; the foyer of the McFinley home was open and majestic, with an Italian chandelier adorning a custom gray marbled floor. Shane and Jill walked through the foyer and through the great room to get to the kitchen. There Shane grabbed two cans of Coke and proceeded poolside. The pool was a beautiful Olympic size pool surrounded by stunning greenery that had been completed by a premier landscaping company in the area. Several lounge chairs accessorized the pool alongside tables with umbrellas, There was also a guest house that was decorated as elaborately as the main house. Stephanie and Jessica had shopped together to ensure every detail was covered when building each of their homes years ago. Shane and

Jill shared many afternoons and evenings at this pool. This evening however, would be a first, as their relationship had progressed to the next level. "Some day, you'll be Mrs. McFinley….that sounds good doesn't it?" said Shane. Jill laughed, "Oh don't go there, don't forget, you still need to talk to my parents…." Shane spoke confidently, "I haven't forgotten, maybe I will talk with them tonight; we need some good news." "It does sound good," Jill concluded. They both smiled and Shane leaned over and kissed Jill. They had barely started their meals; neither of them seeming very hungry Jill held her fork for her salad as Shane lavished kisses on her while running his hands through her shoulder length curls. Jill pulled away from Shane and asked, "Shane, do you think we're moving too fast?" Shane leaned his head against Jill's forehead, "I think that I have held my feelings for you so long, that now it's like a dam breaking….but if you are the least bit uncomfortable, or if you want me to wait to talk to your parents, I'll follow your wishes."

Jill began to tear up. She was so grateful to have Shane as a friend, and now a potential mate. She couldn't imagine life without him. She never considered until now that he would be her life covenant partner. The event today with Granny P made Jill very sentimental. She was reflective and thankful for the people in her life. Shane continued to rub Jill's face and fingers through her hair as a tear drops down her face. Shane wiped her tears with his thumb and continued kissing her. Shane took Jill by the hand and led her into the pool house. He looked in to her eyes and said,

"Jill Richardson, I love you!" . Shane shut the

pool house door behind him.

Chapter Twenty-six

With Stephanie and Carl obviously agreeing

regarding Shane and Jill dating, it was creating a

strange tension at the table. Carl, who was not

really willing to get into a discussion in an open

forum regarding Shane and Jill, grabbed his tray

and broke the silence. "We better check on

Granny P and Selma." Stephanie followed Carl by

pointing out, "Carl I'm in agreement with you

concerning that as well!" Henry followed without

a word, while Jessica was clearly biting her lip

unsure if she would be the odd man out

concerning her opinion of Shane and Jill.

The couples arrived at Granny P's room; the nurse

was in the room checking to make sure she was

comfortable. The nurse politely motioned for the

foursome to stop and everyone backed out of the

door. The nurse came outside of the room. "Mrs.

Perry can't have any visitors right now, are you

her family?" Carl replied, "Yes, we are. My son

told me she had to be revived again." "Yes, that is

correct. We were able to bring her back quickly.

We will be monitoring her closely," said the nurse.

They all thanked her for the update and askd that

she call if there was any change. Jessica and

Stephanie gave their cell phone numbers to the

nurse to put in the file.

The four proceeded to Selma Taylor's room. The couples moved to the next room all without a word. Carl and Henry immediately went on alert looking around when they arrived on the floor, making sure they are ready for another encounter with Cal Taylor. They walked in Selma's room; Courtney and Marcie were sitting on the couch laughing and eating microwave popcorn. Even though everyone was taken by surprise, it was a pleasant surprise. Jessica said, "Alright, a smile! You don't know how glad that makes my heart." "Absolutely!!" chimed Henry. Marcie smiled and held her head down. "If it's okay, can I stay again? Mr. and Mrs. Richardson, I'm so grateful for the offer to stay in your home, but I would really feel better if I stayed here with my mom. The police officer is outside, so that makes me feel a lot more comfortable….please…please…please let me stay." Marcie pleaded. "Well Courtney, is it ok for her to stay here?" asked Jessica. "Since Mrs. Taylor is in a private room, thereis no problem. And, I'm going to be around again tonight. I'llll talk to the lead nurse on duty here on the floor." "Marcie, I will check on you tomorrow. I can call your teachers andyou're your assignments if you would like," said Jessica. "That would be great. You can call the main office at Franklin High, that's where I attend school now." Jessica nodded and said, "I will do just that. I will even go by and pick up anything that's needed." "Thank you so much Mrs. Richardson." Marcie was happy she was going to be able to stay with her mother another night. Going home definitely wasn't an option and she didn't want to feel as if she was a burden to someone else. However, Marcie knew very well that the Richardsons were very sincere in wanting to help her. She was concluding that help is what she needed and she was coming around to accepting it.

Chapter Twenty-seven

The ride from the hospital was aberrantly silent.

Carl and Jessica dropped Henry and Stephanie off

at home just a few streets over from their house.

Their homes are within walking distance of the

others in the influential, gas light lined streets. The

area is like a small city inside a city with village

restaurants and shopping that is convenient for the

residents of Hasbro village. Stephanie's car was

parked out front. Henry took out his keys and

pulled the car in the garage.

Jessica powered the window down and said, "Let Jill know we are here, and you don't have to worry about bringing her home later." Stephanie replied with a simple "yes", and entered the code for the front door. Henry came back to the car, "You two are not coming in tonight?" Jessica said, "I'll pass tonight. I'm done, and my bed would be the best place for me after a long warm bath." Stephanie came to the door to let Jessica know that they were not in the house, and that they may have walked back to their house. They say their good byes.

Carl and Jessica's ride home was silent. Carl even turned off the radio he previously had playing, in an attempt to cut through the tension in the air with Henry and Stephanie. They are all aware of the tension, but refused to speak on it. Carl pulled into the garage at home; lights can be seen from outside of the house, so it's pretty clear that the kids are probably inside.

Just as days gone by, Carl and Jessica walked in from the garage and noise from the television was coming from the family room. Jill and Shane's laughter could be heard over any channel the television was set on. Shane was making Jill laugh hysterically with one of his funny impressions of someone they both knew. As Jessica heard their laughter, she couldn't help but think how Shane could always make Jill laugh. When Carl's father died, Jill was so upset, she refused to eat or come out of her room. Jill was lying in the bed whenShane came over. He went right to her room and within five minutes she could be heard laughing. In no time at all, Shane had Jill dressed and downstairs eating pizza he had picked up on the way over.

Carl yelled out, "Hey kids, I see you two are doing much better." Taking time out from giggling, Jill asked, "Hey Uncle Carl, where is Aunt Jess?" "I'm here," said Jessica. She was a little slower coming around the corner than Carl. "Yeah, we're doing much better. I am doing better only because of Shane. You know he has a knack for making me laugh." Carl said, "I know and I am grateful for it." Shane didn't waste any time moving to the next point. "Uncle Carl and Aunt

Jess can I talk with you for a minute?" Jessica's heart sank. Could Shane be moving to the playing field that she wasn't ready to enter with him and Jill? Jessica took a deep breath and sat down on the edge of her chocolate sectional that filled the family room. Carl was more than happy to talk and resounded with a chipper "Yes, sure son, what's up?"

"You know Jill is my best friend. We do everything together and I tell her everything...." Jessica chimed in so it wouldn't appear that she was too distant. "YES, You are like brother and sister." "....right Aunt Jess we are, Shane continued, "But, things have changed. My love and the feelings I have for Jill are more then that. I want to spend the rest of my life with Jill and would like your permission to date her with that intention in mind." Carl, who was absolutely ecstatic, jumped to his feet, "I knew it! I knew it! I knew it! Well, sir…" Jessica jumped in without thinking about Jill. "What about school you two? Why are you so bent on having a relationship now? Finish school, go off to college and enjoy life!" Shane and Jill were both taken aback by her response. Carl was surprised by her response, but he was more surprised by the tone in which she delivered her concern. It was almost as if she was appalled at seeing them with each other. Jill looked at her mom and said, "Mom, we are sitting right here!" Shane tapped Jill on her leg to indicate that he was okay. "Aunt Jess, we're not getting married tomorrow. We have every intention of finishing school." Jessica still not aware of the tone in her voice said, "OK, well reevaluate how you feel at that time, if you can wait that long, then you know it's worth it." Carl looked at Jessica and said, "Are you serious?" Carl was actually mortified by his wife's response, turned to Shane and said, "Shane not only do you have my approval to date my daughter with the intentions of making her your wife, as her father I also give my blessing." Jill jumped up and hugged her dad. Jessica without another word left the family room.

Chapter Twenty-eight

Courtney brought another blanket for Marcie and a popped bag of popcorn. Popcorn could be smelled throughout the hallways of North General's sixth floor. Selma was finally resting well. Marcie had said her good nights and was preparing her couch for her evening rest. She was clearly opening up and feeling comfortable with Courtney in such a short time. "Marcie, I have to report for my shift in about thirty minutes. You know the guard is outside and they will be changing at about 11:00 or 11:30 p.m. this evening. If you need anything, the nurses at the station will be available, or I'm right down stairs." Marcie replied, "Thank you so much for everything that you have done for my mom and me. I really appreciate it." "Marcie you are welcome…" Courtney thought she would make one more attempt prior to starting her shift to see if she could get the truth from Marcie concerning her home environment. "…can you talk about what happened?" Marcie put the pillow over her face, "Everything is as I mentioned before, but…" Marcie was so full of fear. She had never exposed anyone to her personal life. It was out of fear and embarrassment. Courtney was listening intently in hopes that Marcie would finally share. "…this isn't the first time my father has beat my mother.

It has never been this bad and…I have never been this scared." Tears that Marcie didn't think were left, began to fall. Courtney held her hand "Has your dad ever hit you?" Marcie crying and breathing heavier said, "Yes, and…" just, then a shadow of a man appeared at the front door of the hospital room. Everything moved at the speed of light, Courtney turned, "How did you get in here?!" In one blow, Cal Taylor hit Courtney knocking her out unconscious and onto the floor. Cal in his next move grabbed Marcie with his hand around her mouth before she could let out a scream. Marcie's one hundred and thirty-five pound frame was no match for her father's brute force. Marcie felt her body tensing up as she tries desperately not to allow it to happen. She wanted to fight back, but fear is paralyzing her ability to

184

exchange blows with her once caring and

protective father. Marcie wished Courtney would

wake up; she wished she could retaliate, but her

father has her too tight. Cal dragged Marcie in the

bathroom She smelled the alcohol on his breath as

she had in previous encounters. Cal lifted Marcie's

shirt and bra with one hand. Marcie felt abnormal,

but familiar warmth in the front of her pants she

thinks to herself,

"OH GOD! No!"

Chapter Twenty-nine

Jessica retreated to her second floor office which is just as particular and well decorated as the rest of her home. A large mahogany desk inlaid with calf's leather is the focal point of the office. Fresh cut flowers in a Waterford vase embellish her desk; Carl sends these weekly.. Two custom built mahogany bookshelves flank the walls of the office. Each shelf holds an array of old English literature to the poetry of Maya Angelou.

Jessica rummaged through her hand bag trying to find her cell phone. She was clearly anxious and nervous about what had taken place in her family room. Jessica paced the floor while she tried to dial her intended number. She closed the door listens as the phone rings. "Hi it's Jessica. I need to talk... it's never a good time... you are not the only person shouldering this responsibility..... NO! YOU DON'T UNDERSTAND...listen...I DID, I saw the look in her eyes..... there will be....LOOK, I just need some support here...WHAT...NO, NO I need to think about that.... You are not the only person affected here...well, that is how *you* are acting...NO you weren't..." There is knocking at Jessica's office door. "Jessica we need to talk. It was Carl. "Don't think that staying in that room all night..."

187

"...CARL,I'll be out in a minute..." Jessica

resume her cell phone conversation. "...okay, I

will not be able to talk much longer. WE need to

figure this out...well, I'm not comfortable with

your way of dealing with it. I just think there

could be another way....I don't know, if I had

known I would have handled it by now...yeah,...

okay,.... whatever. Good bye!"

Jessica sat down in the middle of her office floor.

She'snot concerned with her St. John pant suit or

the run in her Dior hosiery. The tears begin to fall.

For the first time, she was full of remorse, fear and

uncertainty.

Chapter Thirty

Jessica, now lying on the floor of her office trying
to hold back from crying uncontrollably. She
didn't want Carl to come to the door, and she
definitely didn't want Jill to hear her. She was in a
place of hesitancy and indecisiveness, which
continue to cause her to weep. Jessica needed the
Lord more than anytime in her life so she thought,
but even in this low state she couldn't bring
herself to call on Him. Her act of wallowing in
self-pity out weighed her making the effort to

open her mouth to surrender in humility. As she

decided to attempt to get herself together, she

looked up and Jill was standing in her office.

Jessica just looked at her, dreading the

conversation they were about to have. "Mom....."

Jill pauses, feeling that she is not sure that she

wants to have the conversation She knew that she

couldn't avoid it. Jill was so humiliated by her

mother's behavior tonight. She wasn't concerned

about Shane's reaction; she was more concerned

about the strain this would be on her relationship

with her mother.

"...Mom,...you and Dad have been together since

you were sophomores in high school. You

graduated, went away to school, finished your BA,

and completed your Masters..." Jessica

interrupted, "Jill, I am well aware of my decisions that I have made..." Jill couldn't believe how her mother is acting.i "...Mom, please...please..." Jill was trying hard to hold back her tears; "...you do all of this with your best friends by your side. Aunt Stephanie, Uncle Henry, you and daddy have been friends with each other for such a long time...years before I was born. Shane and I have grown up together....you know them, and you know Shane well. Please help me understand what was that all about down stairs? Why are you so against Shane and I being together? He even came and asked permission..."

Jessica rose to her feet and made a poor attempt of getting herself together. She pulled a couple of

191

tissues from the box on her desk. "Jill, I can't have this conversation with you right now, I have said all that I have to say…You two need to wait until you finish college. That's all I have to say about it!" Jill resisted her mother's insistence, "Mom, you have to do better than that, you just humiliated me down stairs in front of my best friend and man that looks up to you as if you are his second mother…" said Jill. Jessica lit into Jill, "Oh please, little girl, he is no more a man than you are a woman. You are so busy thinking about your little puppy love affair you don't even think about what this decision will do to those around you. You both are just so concerned with yourselves. How selfish can you be?"

Jill exploded into tears, "How selfish can I be? Mom, what is this really about?…you can't tell me that a decision to make a life long friend a covenant partner, someone I can trust, grow old with, build a family with and fulfill my destiny and purpose in this earth is being selfish…" Jessica began to yell at the top of her lungs through tears and all. Jill had never seen her mother like this. "JILL, I AM TELLING YOU STOP IT! STOP IT! I AM NOT GOING TO TALK ABOUT THIS WITH YOU ANY MORE….JUST STAY AWAY FROM HIM!" Jill was unrelenting, and with just as much volume in her voice took a deep breath and yelled back at her mother, "I WILL NOT STAY AWAY…..I HAVEN'T STAYED AWAY THE LAST SEVENTEEN YEARS AND I AM NOT GOING

TO STAY AWAY NOW…" The whole time Jill was yelling, Jessica was pacing back and forth in her office. At this point, Jessica was shaking from head to toe. She kept mumbling to herself, "no, no, no…" and running her hands through her hair. She appeared to be having a psychotic break.

Jill tried to snap her mother out of whatever issues she was having, "…WHAT IS YOUR PROBLEM? WHAT IS IT ABOUT SHANE THAT HAS CAUSED YOU TO TURN INTO A WOMAN WHO I DON'T EVENKNOW….WHAT IS IT MOM? WHAT IS IT???...." Screaming Jessica cries out,

"JILL….*HE'S YOUR BROTHER!!!!!*

Pre-Order the sequel

"Covenant of Lies the Revealed Truth"

at

www.monarchpublicationsllc.webs.com.

Thank you for purchasing this dynamic book
"Covenant of Lies: The Untold Truth" by
Holly Spence.

For additional copies of *"Covenant
of Lies: The Untold Truth* or other
books written by author Holly
Spence, visit Monarch Publications,
LLC website.

www.monarchpublicationsllc.webs.com

See additional books published by
Author Holly Spence

HOLLY SPENCE

available on audio

*See what others are saying about this
dynamic publication;*

"The heart issues that you describe are right
on...All servants, even those who are leaders
can benefit from preparing a heart to serve."
Dr. Rodney Swope
Rod & Staff Enterprises
www.rodnstaff.net

"We often need a goad to cause us to stop and
take the time to reaffirm our commitment to
Christ and service others as an outflow of that
commitment. This book offers good biblical and
comical anecdotes to cause us to pause in our
journey reflect and readjust our hearts."
Elder Monica Keenon
iSucseed, LLC
isucseed@hotmail.com

"WARNING: WHAT YOU ARE ABOUT TO READ
MAY BE DANGEROUS TO YOUR SPIRTUAL AND
POLITICAL HEALTH!"
Apostle Bennie Fluellen
Overflow Ministries Covenant Church
www.omccministries.com

You've rendered an excellent program of empowerment. Very nicely done! Good flow. Nice overlaps between key topics. I especially liked the areas where you completely turn loose and throw the fire of your personality into it. That fire is "you" and makes the book. Very impressive methodology. Keep it up!

> Larry Trujillo
> Principal Consultant
> Oracle Corporation

I think your book so far is well laid out, easy to read, interactive and engaging. Each chapter I've read, entices me to participate in the process and the activities. It's very applicable to life, not just work.

> Cindy Dutra
> Oracle Corporation

Well, I have a 2-year-old son and a 3.5-year-old daughter and even though they are not in school, I still run around like a chicken with my head cut off. Sometimes you have to take 10 minutes to just calm down, but sometimes Holly, it's not possible. I always worked a 9 to 5 or 9 to 8 before I had kids. I'm trying to get this online business situated, plus my own business situated so I will have more than 10 minutes to relax. I've seen it done, and I see it being done. You know what my 10 minutes consist of? Giving back whether it be advice, whether it just be thanking God for all he has done for me and people who've I've come in contact with. Even though I don't lay my head to rest until 11 sometimes 12, I still feel my mind working. But you have given me something to think about. RELAX, RELATE, RELEASE!

Annie McCall

Workshops are currently being scheduled for corporate entry-level management, senior executives, church leadership and team workshops.

For workshop information and speaking engagement requests, please send an email to monarchpublcaitonsllc@yahoo.com

**See additional books published by
Monarch Publications, LLC**

*"This young lady is spiritually inspired; God has
surely touched her hands…."*
Clyde Lee

*"…yours is providing an avenue for others to self
reflect, so we may see our inner self."*
Sandra Evans

*"…a book that gives you hope and determination
to never give up on yourself…."*
Shelley M. Glaspie

*"… There are not many people who could expose
themselves to such worldwide scrutiny, but you
have done it in such an elegant way as to cause
the reader to examine their own life."*
Elder Samuel Tolble

www.ingramcontent.com/pod-product-compliance
Lightning Source LLC
Chambersburg PA
CBHW070500260626
47161CB00004B/1392